MOMENTS OF TRUTH
STORIES ABOUT NIGHTS WHEN THE LIGHT GETS IN

KEITH McDONALD

Bahá'í Publications Australia
ISBN 978-1-925320-61-9

Printed and Distributed by
Bahá'í Distribution Service of Australia
bds@bahai.org.au
www.bahaibooks.com.au

To Fiona, my love and light in the dark
(especially at 6am in the winter)

People are like stained-glass windows.
They sparkle and shine when the sun is
out, but when the darkness sets in, their
true beauty is revealed only if there is
light from within.
— *Elisabeth Kübler-Ross*

CONTENTS

ESSAYS

LEAP OF FAITH

APART FROM A summer job in a department store when I was still at school, my only paid work has been in journalism. During 44 years as a print journalist I never rose to dizzy heights, but I like to think that in a local context I brought some pleasure to people with a few of my efforts.

It was as a journalist during my cadetship with the Croydon Advertiser in south London in 1971 that I first heard of the Bahá'í Faith. I was working in the Advertiser's Epsom district office at the time. "Office" is a rather grand description of my then workplace. It was literally a single room over a betting shop and next door to a pub in Epsom High Street. It housed five reporters and numerous crumpled files of broadsheet newspapers. People would walk in — there was no front desk or receptionist — with story tips, to place adverts or just to sound off about something. We simply took the ads and sent them over to head office in Croydon.

One day a couple of people walked in with an ad and after they'd left, it was pointed out to me that one of the pair was an actor, Phillip Hinton. Not only that but he was also a member of some religion with an unpronounceable name. He was a Bahá'í, though none of my colleagues knew how to pronounce the word. They made it sound strange. OK, so he was a small-town celebrity. Big deal. There were celebrities more famous than that living in the upmarket Epsom area.

A little while later, I ran into my second Bahá'í. Dave Rose, a big bear of a man, was a reporter on the opposition Herald paper. Yes, there was more than one local newspaper in those days and between us we must have had about 10 journalists covering the area. Halcyon days. Dave was heavily into the music scene, something we had in common, and he invited me to go with him to a gig by a London band called Quintessence in nearby Kingston. Neither of us had a car, so we caught a bus that evening to Kingston. On the way, he told me about the Bahá'í Faith and, far from sounding strange, I found it quite sensible and interesting.

He invited me to a Bahá'í meeting the following week. There, I met up with Phillip Hinton and other local Bahá'ís. Two American Bahá'í musicians, England Dan and John Ford Coley, who were touring the UK, sang and there was an introductory talk about the Faith. The talk confirmed my interest because it sounded very logical and included acceptance of all the other major religions, such as Christianity, Islam and Judaism, rather than claiming to be the only "true" religion, as followers of various religions were often prone to say.

With my interest well and truly captured, I became friends with other Epsom Bahá'ís. I started going to their meetings, most notably a weekly "fireside" in the home of a young family where there would be a talk, games and chat. My social life started revolving around the Bahá'ís, including a number of students from the local art school, and I ventured with trepidation into my first Bahá'í party. The trepidation was on account of there being no alcohol because Bahá'ís don't drink. To my relief and great pleasure, the booze-free party was a revelation. Yes, it was possible to shed inhibitions without the use of alcohol; to open up and talk meaningfully to girls without the motive being primarily sexual.

But there was a problem. I wasn't convinced about the idea of God. A Bahá'í earnestly explained to me that because Bahá'u'lláh, the founder of the Bahá'í Faith, spoke as a "Manifestation of God" and thus with the authority of God, ipso facto God was real. I still wasn't convinced because I hadn't yet accepted Bahá'u'lláh as the return of Christ and fulfillment of all major religious prophecy, so I wasn't ready to accept that argument as proof of God's existence.

Phillip told me, after I had been around Bahá'ís for a few months, that I was like someone sitting at the side of a sparkling blue pool gazing admiringly at the sunlit water but I could never fully enjoy the wonders of the water until I dived into it. In other words, I should become a Bahá'í rather than hedge my bets on the outside of the Faith looking in.

It took me about a year and a half to heed his advice and dive in. That happened when I went with Pat Beer, one of the Epsom Bahá'ís, to a Bahá'í summer school in the Scottish Highlands north of Inverness. I had never travelled that far north and I found the landscape magical, but even more magical was the dazzling spirit of the 50 or so Bahá'ís at the summer school. It was a big moment of truth. God was alive, magic was afoot. On the third day, I took the plunge and signed a declaration card affirming my belief in Bahá'u'lláh as the Manifestation of God for this age. That was all it took to be a Bahá'í.

Not only was that decision one of the biggest moments of my life, but that summer school also introduced me to my future wife, Fiona. She was instrumental in convincing me that I should become a Bahá'í.

Initially, I felt strange being a member of a religion, especially the fact that I was no longer meant to drink alcohol, a mainstay of journalism culture. How could I have any professional credibility as a teetotaller? It took me a few weeks to be comfortable with going to a pub and asking for nothing stronger than a Coke, but from then onwards it was just a normal part of my everyday life and has never caused me any stress.

Phillip and his wife, Ann, were among the inspirational figures in my investigation of the Faith and when Phillip passed away this July at the age of 79, it brought memories of those formative Epsom experiences flooding back into my mind. When I read some of the tributes to him on Facebook, I took strength and inspiration from the way he clearly had influenced so many creative people in their artistic endeavours. That, in turn, motivated me to get this collection of short stories over the finishing line.

I am the master of procrastination, never able to satisfy myself that my work is quite good enough, fearful of failure and too easily distracted by other demands or temptations. That fear of failure is something I probably have in common with many other writers. Even acclaimed American author Ann Patchett suffered from it early in her career. *"While I thought I might publish something someday, I was sure that very few people, and maybe no one at all, would read what I wrote,"* she said in *A Practical Memoir about Writing and Life.* Her subsequent success is reassuring.

Despite the hesitancy that accompanied my writing, especially short fiction, I resolved to jump into the high-risk, snarling sea of public judgment by going ahead and finally publish this first-ever book rather than stay sitting on the beach contorted by self-doubt. It is another important moment of truth for me.

I take heart from these words of Michael Caine, who has faced many moments of truth in his acting career: *"The only way to be sure you never fail is never to do anything at all. And the only way to really, truly fail is not to learn from your failures. Any time you learn from a failure, it's a success."*

Every short story and essay here is Bahá'í-inspired. That's because a huge part of my life has revolved around the Bahá'í Faith and Bahá'ís for almost 50 years and the work here draws on that experience. That is not to say that the book is necessarily about the Faith, but it is written from a Bahá'í perspective. Nor is the book exclusively aimed at just Bahá'ís and others familiar with Bahá'í ideas and the Bahá'í community. Our faith, if we have one, is not something that we can switch on or off at will. It should be the essence of who we are, wherever we go and whatever we do. As St Francis of Assisi said: *"Go into the world to preach the gospel and, if necessary, use words."*

It is a book of stories and essays about the struggle to live better and, in so doing, to serve humanity and help build a better world. My hope is that the stories will appeal to a broad audience, irrespective of whether a person has heard of the Bahá'í Faith.

— Perth, WA, August 2021

SHORT STORIES

FREMANTLE UPS AND DOWNS

Protect these children, graciously assist
them to be educated and enable them to
render service to the world of humanity.
O God! These children are pearls, cause
them to be nurtured within the shell of Thy
loving-kindness.

— 'Abdu'l-Bahá, Prayers

FOUR TIMES THE Ferris wheel took them above the historic city of Fremantle and then down again. Like a phoenix rising slowly from the ashes, he climbed and gazed across to South Beach, where he had swum on hundreds of early mornings, giving each day the best of starts. Then it was back down to earth. Rising again, he stared at the harbour, where he had seen big cruise ships docked regally but also warships and sheep ships. That sinking feeling.

His emotions soared and plunged as the memories of his 40 years in Fremantle went up and down with the wheel. But his granddaughter squealed with delight. For her, the view out the window was all new and exciting; for him, regret stained the pleasure.

He was thinking of the times when he believed he was on the cusp of great things. Fremantle, more than anywhere else that he knew in Western Australia, had embodied hope. So many people here had wanted change. How often he had sat at cafes and meetings with like minds charting the future.

Now most of those people had slipped into the shadows and the conversation today was more of a squabble or, worse, no conversation. Like the story that Fremantle's many abandoned shops told, he felt that his time had gone.

But he was with his granddaughter, so full of excitement and potential, looking forward, not back. He owed it to her to be positive and optimistic.

"Look at that funny boat, Poppy," she shrieked, pointing at the harbour.

"That's a sheep ship," he said.

She laughed with disbelief. "Sheep have a ship?"

"Yes, farmers send some of their sheep to other countries and they go on those special ships."

"Do they have their own rooms?"

"Nope, they don't even get a BAA-throom!"

He smiled and waited for her to laugh, but she didn't notice the joke.

"What? No bathroom?" she asked. "They just wee all over the floor? Yuck."

Yuck indeed, he thought. Whenever a sheep ship was docked at Fremantle and the wind was blowing in his direction, he could smell it even though his house was more than 3 kilometres away. There was no chance of failing to notice it, no mistaking its source.

The sheep ship dropped behind the city skyline as they descended. When their cabin reached the bottom, it stopped and they got out. He and the wide-eyed blonde child walked hand in hand across the park towards the heart of the city. On their right, teenage boys in caps and low-slung pants attempted aerobatics in the skate park.

His granddaughter stared. "Can we go in there?"

"No, we don't have any skateboards," he answered, glad to have a valid excuse, but her disappointment was obvious.

As they neared the hotel across the road from the park, they saw two men slugging it out in a fistfight. He steered his precious cargo away from the ugly scrap.

"Poppy, why are they fighting?"

"Because they're drunk and they're stupid."

He regretted being so harsh — planting his own prejudices in his granddaughter's innocent head — but he didn't know how to repair the damage. Scurrying away as much from his angry words as from the fight, he led her up Essex Street towards the Cappuccino Strip. On the corner of the tourist strip, a group of teenage boys eyed them menacingly as they passed Hungry Jack's, with its intimidating smell of burgers and burning fat.

It was Saturday afternoon and there were lots of people about — the weekend hordes who flocked to Fremantle, the only part of Perth where history had more or less beaten the bulldozers. Not that most of the visitors came primarily to look at the old buildings. They were more interested in eating and drinking, sitting outdoors at cafes, restaurants, pubs and bars. Even though it was mid-afternoon, plates on the crowded tables outside one of these restaurants contained enough food to feed a Third World village for a year.

He was losing the struggle to think positively but at Pizza Bella Roma the sight of tables bulging with pizzas was a temptation his granddaughter couldn't resist. She pleaded with him to buy her pizza. He couldn't resist the chance to spoil her — and buy her some compensation.

There were no empty tables outside so they sat inside … where he remembered he and his wife had once attempted to hold a "family meeting" with their two attitude-fuelled teenage children, as recommended by parenting experts at the time. The kids had felt hijacked and he and his now ex-wife's plan to ram home a few messages failed dismally. He smiled at the memory of another parenting failure. All of them had been his fault, according to his ex.

Across the street at Gino's or the long-gone Papa's, he'd sat with friends of an evening philosophising until closing time when theirs was the only table remaining on the pavement outside the cafes. He smiled at that memory too. Looking back, it had been nothing but idle talk.

"When I grow up, I want to have a pizza shop like this," his granddaughter said, and meant it, as she tucked into the giant pizza they were sharing.

He thought of all the bad-tempered customers she would have at her "shop" and all the useless staff who would treat the customers as the enemy.

"I wouldn't if I were you," he scoffed.

"It'd be so fun," she said.

After the pizza, they walked down High Street to the Roundhouse, which was built in 1831 as a prison for the new colony and was now WA's oldest public building. When tourists visited Fremantle, this was one of the boxes to tick on their itinerary. It had closed for the day.

"What's wrong with this country? Why do they shut so damn early? I've come all the way from Britain to see this and it's closed! People here haven't a clue!"

The fat English tourist was loudly broadcasting his disdain to anyone within about 50 metres. The aggrieved local and his granddaughter looked at each other. He raised his eyebrows and pulled a face. He couldn't stand tourists who thought the whole world had to dance to their tune. If he hadn't had his granddaughter with him, he would have told the guy that they deliberately shut early to keep out ugly, fat Poms.

"He could always come back tomorrow," she said, seeing a solution where the Englishman could see only grievance.

But she didn't dwell on the angry man. She was far more interested in the building itself. It was round and she had never seen one that shape.

"I want to live in a round house," she said, determined rather than wishful. "A big, huge round house. As big as the wheel in the sky."

"They wouldn't let you build something like that in Freo," he said. "They don't like tall buildings here."

"Well, I'd just build it and not tell them until it was done."

"Things are not that simple in the adult world, sweetie."

"They should let us kids run things."

"That's not such a bad idea."

They walked in silence back to his car. Maybe her imagination had taken her away and she was busy making plans for that giant round house; he was trying to imagine what the world would look like through a child's eyes. A world free of addiction to tunnel vision, intolerance or disappointment and full of youthful hope. A child too young and naive to be cynical; too idealistic to let reality get in the way.

Through his granddaughter's eyes, he could see Fremantle as a wonderland of possibility, the way he used to see it, and not the wasteland of abandoned dreams it had become for him.

"You know, sweetie, it's as if adults have been cemented into the ground." She looked up blankly at him. "And we envy you kids because you can fly free into the sky. I just wish you could keep flying for the rest of your life and not have your wings clipped."

She considered his words for a moment.

"What wings?" she asked.

SAINT AND SINNER

O Lord, Thou possessor of infinite mercy!
O Lord of forgiveness and pardon! Forgive our
sins, pardon our shortcomings, and cause us to
turn to the kingdom of Thy clemency, invoking
the kingdom of might and power, humble at
Thy shrine and submissive before the glory of
Thine evidences.

— 'Abdu'l-Bahá, Prayer

SORAYA WAS WAITING for Jacquie, ennobled by six giant columns, on the steps of St Martin-in-the-Fields in London's Trafalgar Square. Her long black hair was gathered in immaculate defiance of the wind's assaults. This meeting hadn't been on Jacquie's radar until about 5.30. The shock of what she'd discovered that afternoon sent her scurrying for an escape. Fellow Australian Soraya was the first person she thought of as she ran from the wreckage of her marriage — she was her nearest harbour, her place of refuge. Now Jacquie arrived bedraggled and aching.

When Jacquie had rung her, Soraya was just about to leave work in central London and Jacquie could almost see her jigging with excitement at hearing from her. She was always so bubbly. Jacquie — who hadn't seen her friend for more than a year, not since Soraya left Australia to work in London — had explained that her husband, Stuart, was busy with his family and she wanted some company for the evening. Soraya had offered to come to her in Croydon, 20km south of central London, from where she was phoning, but Jacquie had assured her that she really wanted to come up to the city. She wanted to trade her bland suburban sentence for some big-city distraction. Forty-five minutes later, she was weaving through the crowds of ambling tourists and homeward-bound workers in Trafalgar Square as she approached the church.

"I've missed you," Soraya said, kissing her on each cheek and hugging her. "It's so lovely to see you. It's been too long."

"I've missed you too," Jacquie said, gripping her friend's shoulders as if she were a lifebuoy.

They skimmed over the conversation entrees — Soraya's job, Jacquie's stay in England, how things were back in Perth and, in particular, Soraya lavished sympathy on Jacquie over her recent miscarriage, even though they had thoroughly explored that dark pit over phone and email.

Jacquie explained that she was trying to come off antidepressants and Soraya thought that was a good move because she didn't want to be on them for the rest of her life.

"Yes, but I've been feeling nauseous and had a couple of panic attacks. I'm learning to manage the panic but I have to be careful. I've been fighting it on the way here tonight. The crowds got to me."

"You poor thing. Do you want to go somewhere quiet?"

"I need to eat. My head's spinning. Is there somewhere close by?"

Soraya laughed and said they were standing right next to some stairs that led down into the church's Cafe in the Crypt.

"It's one of the quietest cafes in London."

Jacquie readily agreed. She had taken a battering and couldn't face a lot of walking. Battling the rush-hour crowds at Victoria station and on the Tube, she had started regretting her decision to head into the city but seeing Soraya made it worthwhile because she needed a friend tonight. Especially one like Soraya who didn't burden you with her troubles — probably, it seemed to Jacquie, because she had none.

As soon as the softly lit Crypt opened up before her, she felt calmer. Rows of stone pillars supported bricked arches which curved into a ceiling embedded with hundreds and hundreds more bricks. It was like fountains shooting a spray of water into the air. Beneath it all there were candlelit tables. Instantly, Jacquie felt like she was in the bosom of the church, calmed by its heartbeat and warmth.

They were served their meals at the counter — Soraya spinach and ricotta quiche, Jacquie beef stroganoff — and sat down at a table against a side wall. There was no one at the neighbouring tables. Soraya asked what Jacquie had done that day and she created a "nothing much" smokescreen. Certainly nothing about what had really happened. She looked across the table at Soraya and smiled. Soraya, whose parents were Iranian, looked more beautiful than ever. The innocence of her early 20s was evolving into glowing assurance. She was her one close friend, other than Steph, who was openly religious and happy to talk about it. Jacquie wanted to ask her something. Twice recently Jacquie had prayed out of desperation with more than her usual limp conviction and both times she had felt something like spiritual respite.

"Do you believe that if we pray for help, God answers us?" Jacquie asked.

"Oh, yes, but not always the way we want!"

"I said many prayers for my unborn daughter and then I had the miscarriage. What do you make of that?"

Soraya told her she wasn't God and was reluctant to offer some kind of definitive answer. Jacquie persisted and reluctantly Soraya responded.

"We pray and if terrible things happen, it's easy to blame God, but I don't think God actively decides you will have a miscarriage. It was your body rejecting the baby, not something God instigated. It's incredibly hard." She put down her fork and took one of Jacquie's hands in both of hers across the table. "Even though your daughter has passed away, I believe her soul lives on in the next world and it's good to pray for her progress."

"What about praying to her for help? Or praying to my father-in-law? He died just a week ago. That's why we're here — for his funeral." Jacquie pulled her hand away from Soraya. "Do you think it's possible that prayers reach them and they can respond?"

"Absolutely. I'm sorry about Stuart's dad. You must tell me more about him. I often have my aunt in my prayers. She was arrested in Iran simply for being a Bahá'í and executed almost 30 years ago, before I was born. I sometimes call on her when I need help with something."

Jacquie tried to lighten the conversation.

"Do you ask her to find you a husband?"

Soraya laughed and gave Jacquie a gentle pretend slap on the side of her face.

"I leave all those prayers to my mother."

"Has there been an answer to her prayers yet, Soraya?"

Soraya coyly shook her head.

"Do you believe in forgiveness?" Jacquie asked, growing serious again. Soraya did. "Have you forgiven the people who killed your aunt?"

"I'm working on that," was all she said in reply. She seemed uneasy having to admit that she had not yet been able to forgive.

Her friend's discomfort enticed Jacquie to open up about what had really happened that morning: her own discomfort. With Soraya in this place of sanctuary, she was starting to feel calm and safe, ready to share what had shattered her. She told her how an aunt of Stuart's had accidentally let slip that he had had a younger sister who died tragically in a car accident when she was just five years old and with Stuart at the time — something Stuart had never disclosed to her. This had left her feeling betrayed and humiliated.

"How can a husband not tell his wife something so important? How could his family connive to keep it from me, his wife? I should probably forgive Stuart but I don't know whether I can, even though it might destroy our marriage if I don't. What do you think I should do?"

Soraya didn't answer for a few seconds. She looked troubled.

"Dear, gorgeous Jacquie, I can't tell you what to do but if it were me, I wouldn't want to lose my husband over this. It's probably something very painful for him and maybe he couldn't bring himself to share it with you. Men often flounder with emotional subjects. Many men who fought in the Second World War never spoke about it. Forgiveness doesn't always come easily though. It takes time. I should know."

"So, basically, you think we should kiss and make up?"

"It's not that easy, my gorgeousness. I'm hardly the best person to talk about how to forgive and I'm not married either, so I'm not well qualified to answer you but I would just suggest you hang in there. Marriage requires perseverance. Don't cast it aside as if you were just tossing a piece of waste paper in the garbage bin."

"I only said this might destroy our marriage. I didn't say it definitely would. I didn't say I wanted to leave him."

That rebuke was harsh considering Jacquie had actually made it clear she might be about to destroy her marriage, but Soraya chose not to argue the point.

"OK, I'm sorry. I shouldn't have assumed a worst-case scenario. I'm sorry."

Soraya looked distressed by her "mistake". For a few seconds, they sat in silence. Then Soraya took Jacquie's hands gently in hers — she had always been so tactile — and spoke softly, almost confidentially.

"I think you should pray very hard — I'll pray for you too."

"You'll pray?" Jacquie delivered her surprise in a markedly louder voice. "But you have a different God to mine!"

Soraya laughed so loudly that people turned to look at her.

"We may have different religions but there's only one God."

"So that's why you don't have a problem going with me to this church? I wondered why you'd suggested meeting here."

"I love this place. I often come here. They also have some beautiful concerts upstairs in the church most nights. I come sometimes. There's something on tonight — do you want to go?"

Jacquie liked the idea. "As long as it's not hymn singing, I'm up for it," she replied.

"No, it's Carmina Burana. Do you know it?"

Jacquie had to admit that she didn't. Soraya was so much smarter than her. She was embarrassed at her inadequacies.

"You'll love it," Soraya enthused.

They asked at the box office next to the café for the cheapest seats but only the most expensive were left, on the end of the front row.

Jacquie made to walk away but Soraya insisted on taking the tickets and paying for them herself. Jacquie tried to dissuade her. She was embarrassed at her generosity but Soraya wouldn't listen. When they found their seats, they were shocked to be positioned almost within touching distance of a big choir. As the pair, arm in arm, took their seats and realised they were virtually de facto choristers, they giggled like teenagers.

"Have you ever sung in a choir?" Soraya asked.

"In church, yes. What about you?"

"Yes, I'm in a Bahá'í choir."

"Well, we're ideally qualified then!"

"We've got five minutes to learn our parts!"

As she said this, Soraya opened a copy of the program, which had all the lyrics to Carmina Burana. Jacquie warbled the opening lines in a mock soprano imitation.

A couple of metres away a member of the choir looked at her and smiled.

"We're one short tonight. Do you want to step up?" the elderly man joked.

They giggled again.

The concert started with a jazz quartet. It seemed unusual to have modern music played in such a grand and iconic 300-year-old church. Jacquie thought back to her father-in-law's funeral a day earlier and how moribund that church had seemed. By contrast, St Martin's was bubbling with life.

After the intermission, it was Carmina Burana. Sitting so close to the choir and musicians, Jacquie could physically feel the force of the explosive opening movement. The exuberant music was powerful but sitting so close to it was electrifying. Even the quieter passages, where the full choir wasn't singing, still kept suspended above the despair of the day.

At the end, she clapped ecstatically, saying, "O my God, that was unbelievable." Then, as the audience's clapping subsided, she sank, overcome, into Soraya's shoulder and cried. The elderly chorister gently touched her on the shoulder and said quietly: "Music can be so emotional."

It took Jacquie a couple of minutes to show her tear-streaked face and she nestled in Soraya's embrace. By then most of the audience had gone and some of the choir and orchestra were moving away.

"O no, my mascara's made a mess of your jacket. I'm so, so sorry."

"Don't worry about it!" Soraya said, showing no concern whatsoever and taking Jacquie by the hand. "Have you got enough time to say some prayers with me?"

Jacquie checked her watch. Yes, she had time. She'd never wanted to pray as much as she did now. First, though, she asked if they could just sit in silence for a few moments. She could still hear the music and feel the rush of breath from the choir. She wanted to savour it. The soft rattle of conversations in the emptying church failed to intrude. So did the sound of musical equipment being moved out. Then, gradually, as the church grew quieter, Jacquie's thoughts moved beyond the music to wonder what Stuart was doing and thinking. She wondered whether she had it in her to refloat their relationship. Her thoughts developed into a barely uttered prayer.

"God, give me strength to rise above this wild ride. Give me the courage not to give up. Give me the vision to see my way through the difficulties. Thank you, Lord, for giving me such a wonderful friend as Soraya. I pray too for Stuart that he can understand why I am hurting so much. Amen."

There was a long pause. Then Soraya took her Bahá'í prayer book from her handbag and softly sang a prayer: "*O God, refresh and gladden my spirit. Purify my heart. Illumine my powers. I lay all my affairs in Thy hand. Thou art my Guide and my Refuge. I will no longer be sorrowful and grieved; I will be a happy and joyful being. O God, I will no longer be full of anxiety, nor will I let trouble harass me. I will not dwell on the unpleasant things of life. O God, Thou art more friend to me than I am to myself. I dedicate myself to Thee, O Lord.*"

When Soraya finished, Jacquie gazed at her. Her eyes were closed. Then Jacquie slowly looked up at the huge window in the back of the church. Instead of stained glass, it was clear with black lines running vertically and horizontally. In the middle, a glowing egg shape blocked the way and the lines bent around it.

Soraya opened her eyes and, seeing Jacquie looking at the window, asked her if she liked it.

"Yes, it's quite hypnotic considering it's such a basic design."

"It reminds me of an oasis of calm or a point of light surrounded by confusion and turbulence."

Jacquie laughed.

"It's like my life tonight. Calm amid a storm."

OFF THE RAILS

O Ye Rich Ones on Earth! The poor in your
midst are My trust; guard ye My trust, and
be not intent only on your own ease.
— Baha'u'llah, Hidden Words

IT WAS LESS than a week after the winter solstice and overcoat-scarf-and-beanie cold. Yet the sky was blue and the sun was shining, giving a pretence of summer. Out the train windows, trees shorn of their leaves waved defiantly. As the train crossed a bridge into the station, people scuttled around the shops below like ants. One or two people got off the train and more replaced them. It was the tail-end of the morning peak-hour rush so there were a few empty seats, although some passengers preferred to stand.

Then the train moved off again. Three more stations to Flinders Street. More sights to ponder out the window. Yet virtually no one seemed to be watching the passing parade. Their thoughts seemed to be in other places. They weren't actually here in the train! Heavily wrapped against the cold outside, they were also wrapped around their phones, emailing, texting, scrolling through social media messages, playing games or distracting themselves with video clips. Some had headphones or earphones, listening to podcasts or conducting conversations with unseen people in unknown places.

Most in this carriage were almost certainly making their regular commute to work and they didn't need to look out the window because they knew already what was there. They ignored the spectacularly huge and vivid painting of three people filling the end of a two-story building next to the railway line. A black man with two white women, in bed and all clad in bikinis. Seen without warning, it asked questions. What was it about? Were they people who live, or lived, in that building? They looked familiar — maybe one of the women was Taylor Swift. How did the artist manage to paint it on such a tall "canvas"? Then there was all the graffiti passing unobserved along the side of the railway, no wall immune from the scattergun approach of street art.

No one looked up at the apartment blocks glowering reproachfully over the next station and wondered what was happening behind all those empty windows. People thinking of suicide or making love instead of making it to work; someone slowly dying. Pondering such possibilities just required some imagination but technology had taken imaginations hostage in this train.

No one was watching the beautiful young woman with long blonde hair sitting next to the window transfixed by happenings on her phone. Was her beauty only skin deep? Surely a young man — or an old one — could look at her and dream of finding out the answer?

No one wondered how that perspiring man standing next to the door talking to an invisible colleague on his phone and drinking coffee had managed to get so overweight.

In this carriage of perhaps 50 people, how many propelled themselves with silent grief or joy? The middle-aged woman sitting opposite smiling at her phone – was she smiling at a loving text message from her husband or a funny video, "You'll never believe what happens next … "?

Was the man with a face of grim determination across the aisle from her sending a vitriolic message to the woman who had just left him or prepping for an important business meeting in half an hour?

Then a beggar got on.

He was a tall man fighting a losing battle to stand tall. Probably about 50, with all his earthly possessions in two plastic bags. He was wearing old sandals and a dirty brown raincoat held together loosely with a piece of string around his waist. Unkempt grey hair stuck out furiously from under a battered red Nike cap that might well have been retrieved from a rubbish bin. Everyone could smell him from some distance away. He surely wasn't equipped to survive winter nights in Melbourne living on the streets. It was warmer in the trains. He lurched past those standing around the doors, brushing roughly against some and holding an angry conversation with his inner demons. Now people on the train were jolted back to reality and away from their smartphones, wary of this threat to their privacy. Women peeked nervously in his direction. People stepped aside to let him through. Then he stopped and jabbed a man sitting in an aisle seat.

"Give me $5 for a coffee, mate."

It wasn't a question. The man looked indignantly at the beggar.

"Certainly not!"

"Well, up yours, you mongrel!"

He turned to a young woman of about 17 or 18 in another aisle seat. She tugged her black coat tighter around the throat as if to defend herself. Her attempt to look engrossed in her phone gave her no protection.

"Can you spare something? I've got no home, no money, no job. It's not a lot to ask."

He'd put on more of a performance this time, less aggression but still an implied threat that rejection wouldn't be well received. The young woman was a confusion of nervousness and sympathy. Eyes and ears were on her. She reached for the purse in her handbag and gave him the smallest note that she had, $10. He snaffled it eagerly.

"God bless ya, love!"

As he moved on to try his luck with other passengers, the expensively dressed young man sitting next to the teenager reprimanded her.

"Giving him money only encourages him, you know," he said loudly. "You really shouldn't have done that. It was stupid. He'll only spend it on grog or worse."

She looked humiliated; as if she was a first-year student being told off by the school principal in front of all her classmates. She didn't say anything and tried to hide her embarrassment by returning to her phone. The man grunted disapproval and went back to his phone. No one else said anything but she could feel a chorus of silent condemnation.

"Just gave 10 bucks to a beggar on the train," she wrote in a text to her friend. "Got told off by some loser guy"

She finished it with six sad Emojis.

By the time the train reached the next stop, her friend had replied: "The moron!!!!"

"Don't give & you get sworn at, give something & you still get abused! Can't win! Again!!!"

"That sexist pig should have told the tramp to nick off and leave you alone"

Angry Emojis added a few more unspoken words.

"Don't need a man to fight my battles"

"I wouldn't mind one"

 "But I wanted to give him something. Felt sorry for him!"

"Wuss!"

"Whatever. I failed again."

By now the beggar had moved to the far end of the carriage and everyone had returned to their alternative reality. The train slid slowly past the MCG, Australian sport's holiest of holies, on one side of the track, and the Rod Laver Arena facing it on the other side. No one looked wistfully out the train window and remembered going to the tennis at the Arena back in the summer when it was so hot sitting in the sun watching Federer and Williams making world news. Now the tennis complex was deserted, abandoned.

An executive — his suit bulging out of an unbuttoned overcoat — talked on the phone to his partner, trying to patch up things with her after a row and oblivious to the public nature of his remorse. Not that anyone was probably listening to him.

Now they were at Flinders Street station and the young woman spilled out of the train with the other passengers and her text conversation.

"Don't be sad, he's not worth it"

"He was spunky"

"You didn't tell me he was hot!!! Gotta go. Seeya!!"

A much older woman followed her off the train. She wasn't a commuter; she didn't have a job. She had commuted on this line many times from her home in Frankston in the days when she worked in the city at the Myer department store but today she was on her way to her monthly catch-up over coffee and cake in a restaurant at her old workplace with three other women, all former work colleagues. Not having a smartphone or anything to read, she had been sitting behind the young woman — well, girl really, she now realised — and staring at nothing in particular. She'd heard the young man telling off the girl and was appalled at the way he spoke to her. She'd turned and stared in his direction intending to let him know that he should have more respect. But she felt he was arrogant and self-righteous and feared that he would say something much worse to her.

Only a few weeks ago, on the saddest day of her life, she had finally given in and moved her husband into a care home. She was brittle; much more so than she used to be. It wouldn't take much of a verbal bruising from that young man to have her in tears and everyone looking at her. So, she said nothing. She couldn't recognise the woman she had become.

Now, as she walked behind the girl, guilt was engulfing her like rising floodwater. She should have said something. Someone should have let that young man know his behaviour wasn't acceptable, but nobody said a thing. Although she'd lost sight of him in the crowd making for the exit, she was rapidly catching up to his victim who was walking slowly as she texted. She could at least give this girl some moral support. Reaching within touching distance of her, she tapped her on the shoulder. The girl turned around abruptly like a deer about to be hit by a car. Seeing this old woman, her apprehension disappeared.

"What?" she asked aggressively.

"I heard what that young man said to you on the train."

"I hope you're not going to tell me he was right and I'm just a stupid cow."

The older woman was taken aback that this girl would expect such a thing.

"No, no, not at all. The very opposite, in fact. I just wanted to let you know that you didn't deserve that. You did a kind thing and don't deserve to be condemned for a good deed. I thought you were probably upset about what happened and I guess I just wanted to let you know that I'm on your side."

"Oh." As they stood facing each other in the crowd an awkward silence hung between them like a glass wall. "Hmmm, I'm not used to people taking my side," she continued after a long pause. "I'm sorry. I don't know how to handle that."

"Let's just give each other a hug," the older woman said with a smile and opened her arms to embrace her.

As her hands closed in on the girl's shoulders, the girl backed away hurriedly with a flustered, "I'm sorry but thank you." And she scurried off towards the exit. The much-needed hug was left hanging.

ETERNITY: INFINITY IN THE PALM OF YOUR HAND

Bahá'í marriage is the commitment of the
two parties one to the other, and their mutual
attachment of mind and heart. Each must,
however, exercise the utmost care to become
thoroughly acquainted with the character of
the other, that the binding covenant between
them may be a tie that will endure forever.
Their purpose must be this: to become loving
companions and comrades and at one with
each other for time and eternity...
— 'Abdu'l-Bahá, Selections From the Writings

TRACEY SAW GOD in everything. In the food she ate, the people she met. Even when things went against her, God was "testing"
her and it was a way for her to "grow". It frightened off would-be
boyfriends because when a girl's in love with God, it's hard for a guy
to compete against that sort of opposition.

She owned a café and a few days after the long Christmas-New Year break, Sean visited it for the first time on the way back to his office a couple of streets away. He came back every day that week. It wasn't the coffee that drew him back; it was Tracey. Heart-shaped face; long black hair arranged differently every day — one day a ponytail, another day hanging loose, another day pointing skywards. And the way she glided elegantly around the floor of the café — he could happily watch her magnificent derriere undulating hypnotically past his table. Only about 5-foot tall but owning every inch of the café's space — and Sean's attention.

When he returned the following Monday, he had smartened up. The crumpled T-shirt had been replaced with a crisp, ironed white business shirt. He even combed his hair before he went to her café. He wanted to be noticed. He fiddled meaninglessly with his mobile phone, using it as an alibi to try and conceal his visual stalking of Tracey. She was attractive in all the necessary departments. He would have preferred her to have short blonde hair but had developed a new appreciation of long black hair this past week. Beyond the obvious physical attractions, however, her way of smiling and making conversation with the customers — all of them — really hooked him.

She talked to him as if he'd been going in there for years, not just six days. She said something about the weather because it was a perfect summer's day, dazzlingly bright blue, cloudless sky and just 30 degrees, and she was happy. "Isn't it a gorgeous day today?" she said with great relish.

He countered cynically: "It won't last. It'll probably snow tomorrow." As if it ever snowed in Perth! But far from dampening her enthusiasm, the thought of snow made her even happier. "Oh, it'd be fantastic to see the city covered in snow. I've never seen snow. Have you?"

Sean had seen it too many times for his liking. It froze everyday life into a state of paralysis, made driving anywhere a suicide mission and his sister bizarrely held him personally responsible for the weather. He explained that he was Irish and moved to Perth with his family when he was 16. But to his surprise, it felt like Tracey had just blanketed his natural instinct for cynicism with a heavy downfall of the snow she so longed to see. That image came to him as he sat drinking his long black, while she attended to another customer, and he smiled at this sudden poetic turn. Poetry wasn't his thing.

Working the coffee machine, Tracey watched him at the table next to the counter and saw a smile rise over the rim of his cup. And he didn't appear to be smiling at something on his phone. It made her smile; made her go over, when there was a lull in the coffee-making, and talk with him.

Sean came back every day that second week as well. Each time they talked. Sean had a well-honed ability to find out if a girl was (a) single, (b) unattached and (c) straight, and by this second week she had ticked all the right boxes. So, on his tenth visit, Sean invited her to see a reggae band in Fremantle, although he fully expected a brush-off — well, she was too beautiful and smart for the likes of him. He was surprised, therefore, when she said yes: "Oh, that would be so cool. I'd love to."

Not only was the music great, but Tracey was even more into it than Sean. For his part, he couldn't take his eyes off her; couldn't believe his luck. She wasn't particularly glammed up — blue jeans, red V-neck, short-sleeve shirt, regulation make-up — and she wasn't overtly sexy. What transfixed him was how she danced as if it was as natural as breathing and how her smile lit up her face. Even when he watched her walk to the toilet, surely not one of life's moments for supreme artistry, she moved with the grace of a trained dancer. Simple delights.

Even though Sean loved reggae, he was a hopeless dancer. "You look like you've got lead in your boots," Tracey joked, nudging him gently in the ribs. She offered him a lesson in how to lighten up his dancing feet. He didn't feel put down at all and happily accepted. By the end of the gig, Sean was moving much more freely. It hadn't felt like a lesson at all.

Afterwards, they went down the road to Gino's for a coffee, sitting at a table on the pavement within touching distance of the passing late-night revellers. It was the oldest, most famous café in Fremantle and Tracey said it was her favourite. He happily accepted her professional judgment. They talked about the band, about reggae, about the drunk who fell over while he was dancing, about how to make a good cup of coffee and about how the caffeine would keep them awake all night. Sean hoped this was a sign that Tracey planned to spend the night awake with him.

Then, completely out of left field, she went all serious on him: "You know, music can be a ladder to the soul. The right kind of music can take you right out of yourself and to God."

Sean hesitated. He wasn't religious and the closest he got to a religious experience with music was watching Norah Jones singing Come Away With Me. But that was a different kind of religion.

"Wow," said Sean, lost for words and looking idly across the café. "Do you believe in God?"

Sean was tempted to answer: "If He looks like Norah Jones, I do." Luckily, he checked himself. If he gave the wrong answer, he figured that would likely mean going home alone and maybe the end of a beautiful romance before it had even started. But the right answer would probably require Sean to lie. He'd done that before in order to sleep with a girl, but the next morning, after the sex, he always wondered whether it had been worth the moral price as his Irish Catholic inner voice nagged at him. And this time it would require him to sound authentic talking about religion, a task for which he was massively unqualified. Faced with a no-win situation, he tried evasion.

"I believe in something but I don't know if I would call it God."

A smile returned to Tracey's face. "I bet you've never had to tell a girl whether you believe in God on your first date."

Sean took heart that she viewed this as a date and he smiled too, despite the tricky direction their conversation was taking. "No, I haven't. But you know something — it beats the usual first date conversations."

"Oh, how do they usually go?"

"Predictably, often awkwardly."

"Well, God's very unpredictable but is important to me and I want to be clear about that from the outset."

"Wow," said Sean. "That's telling me!" Not that he knew exactly what she was telling him.

"And there's something else that I want to be upfront about. I'm a Bahá'í and I've never slept with a guy."

"Oh no, you don't sleep with girls, do you?" Immediately, Sean regretted what he'd said.

"Oh, haha," said Tracey. Her smile had vanished. "What I mean is, Bahá'ís don't have sex outside of marriage."

"Wow."

"Will you stop saying wow?" Tracey tried to say it lightly but her irritation showed.

"Fair enough. I'm sounding like a wowser. A wow too far. OK, let's talk about sex instead. You don't do it? At all?"

"No. Not until I'm married. I bet you've never had a girl say that to you before on a first date either."

She was dead right there. Sean took stock. On their first date, he had discovered that Tracey was (a) a virgin, (b) didn't do sex before marriage, (c) was hardline religious and (d) probably required any boyfriend to be as obsessed with God as she was. It was a lot to digest over a cup of coffee; more than enough for your average guy, and Sean was tempted to put on his running shoes. But for reasons he couldn't fully explain, he wasn't giving up just yet. There was something indefinable about this girl that made it worth persevering … just as long as she didn't try to convert him. And maybe her no-sex rule wasn't as non-negotiable as she made it sound.

So they survived that first no-sex date and started seeing each other a lot, doing nothing more physically intimate than pecks on the cheek and holding hands. He did try to break her resistance — what guy wouldn't? — but whenever his hand strayed, it was smartly removed. It felt weird at first for Sean, being so puritanical. It was like he had stepped into a Jane Austen book. Not that he had ever read any of her books, but he imagined that she would never have dared to put any of her young unmarried characters in bed with each other. But after a few of these no-sex dates, and realising that there was no chance of Tracey relenting, he began to accept her rules. His desire to get her into bed, whilst still a hope, was no longer an all-important issue. Instead, he experienced a different kind of intimacy, talking openly about problems in his life such as his difficult sister and the wrench of leaving all his friends in Ireland. He'd never really broached these sensitive subjects. Tracey led him into these untraversed backroads and this, in turn, encouraged him to probe her about delicate personal issues such as the impact of her father walking out on her family when she was still at primary school.

One evening in early March, with summer hotly defying the arrival of autumn, Tracey said she wanted to walk on the beach. "I love the beach at night," she said. Sean had never walked anywhere that wasn't totally necessary — like from his bedroom to the toilet or from his office to the carpark. He even drove the 200 metres from his office to Tracey's café. But he agreed. Well, he reasoned, it was something different and quite romantic too, walking hand in hand along the beach in the dark on a warm night with the ocean lapping at their feet. He could handle that. They walked slowly for two hours from North Fremantle to Cottesloe and back. The walk was about one and three-quarter hours longer than he had expected. At first, when Tracey showed no desire to turn back after a few minutes, Sean started to regret agreeing to this but he didn't say anything. Soon, however, he relaxed and thoroughly enjoyed the intimacy of being alone in the dark with Tracey, comfortable with their arms around each other as they walked and talked or just walked in silence, listening to the murmuring approval of the ocean.

It was another new experience for him and later at home alone, as he reflected on his evening with the sound of the sea still in his head, it occurred to him that his warming to the idea of a long walk was very much like his warming to the idea of Tracey herself. He'd never been with a girl like her. She thought differently, did things differently, and he was surprised at how well he was adapting to this different, no-sex type of relationship.

Another time, on another warm evening, she took him to some swings in a park and as they swung back and forth for an hour, they talked about all sorts of things Sean had never talked about before with a girl. Things like fulfilling your potential, capitalism, greed, coffee beans, netball, death and raising children. And religion, but on this subject he just listened and remained non-committal. A couple of times she invited Sean to Bahá'í meetings so that he could hear about her faith, but each time he made excuses not to attend.

This was frustrating for Tracey. She had dated boys, usually fellow Bahá'ís with whom she had grown up, and she had been uncomfortable with the thought of friendships like those turning into a romance. One other boyfriend wasn't a Bahá'í but he lost interest when he found out about her no-sex rule. She wanted to marry and have children but it had been a barren few months for dates and she had turned reluctantly to dating apps. She had attracted interest from some boys but their online or phone chats floundered when Tracey made it clear there would be no one-night stands. Her mother felt it was a mistake to tell them that before she had even met them but Tracey was adamant that the right boy would not be deterred.

Sean had passed the no-sex test. Admittedly, he had tried quite a few times to tempt her into a change of thinking. Once he slid a hand up under her shirt and got as far as her breast. For one delirious moment she had done nothing to remove the hand but then her head took control of her heart.

"Now, now, Sean. You know I don't want you to go there."

She tugged his arm out of her shirt with a playful wag of the index finger on her other hand. He smiled in defeat.

"I'm sorry, Trace, but temptation wouldn't be called that if it was easy to resist."

"It's hard for me too. Please don't make it any harder."

"Well, it's real hard for you right now."

He grinned and looked down at his pants, making it very obvious what he meant. Tracey tried unsuccessfully to hide her embarrassment by laughing at his joke but quickly changed the subject by pointing out two police officers on the other side of the street, joking with an inebriated woman. Sean's defeat was complete.

Despite the odd little tussle like that, Tracey really liked Sean. Really liked. He was fun, considerate, showed surprising depth when he talked about the challenges he had faced in his life and, best of all, was clearly very smitten with her. Yes, he wasn't the sort of boy she had ever imagined herself going for but she was enjoying having her preconceptions dismantled. But there was one very big problem: she just couldn't envisage their relationship going to the next level if he had no interest in her faith. This was a passion, not just a badge or a tribe, and a partner who understood that, and shared it, was essential.

The guys at the designer kitchen business, where Sean was a sales consultant, took persistent interest in Sean's mystery girlfriend. They knew he was seeing someone but they had not met her and Sean had given them only a crumb or two of information. Sean didn't reveal that she owned a nearby café for fear that they would pester her and ruin his reputation. It became an office obsession trying to goad him every day into sharing what sex with his new girlfriend was like. He tried to fob them off but lack of detail didn't stop their fertile imaginations from turning him and Tracey into sexual gymnasts, the subject of constant poor-taste jokes. For probably the first time, this kind of talk irritated Sean, even though he had not previously been averse to making similar crude intrusions into others' relationships. It's what blokes do, was his justification. Now that he'd found a girl he cared about, and who had shown him a different way, he didn't like the crudity but he knew that reacting badly to it, insisting that it was unacceptable, would only make it worse. So he needed to find another way to man up; to set a different kind of example. That was new territory for him

Then came something he'd been dreading: as had happened before, one of the guys organised a Sunday afternoon barbecue at his place and everyone at work — wives and girlfriends included — was invited, especially "Sean's Wonder Woman". In fact, he suspected that the whole thing was a set-up so the boys could meet Tracey. There was no escape; not going wasn't an option. He'd have to take Tracey. She was a factory legend without anyone at work even having met her and now they would inevitably find out about her café and start hounding her there. It would look bad if he and Tracey didn't go but he wondered how could he possibly drop her into something like this, knowing that they'd given her an utterly inappropriate reputation as some kind of sex goddess? He'd not told her the things that had been said about them at work — how could he? The possibility of that being exposed was bad enough but even worse for him was the prospect of Tracey going all religious on people at the barbecue. Then he'd never hear the end of it at work after that. Sean reasoned that it would be a good time for her God to show Himself and save them.

Sean's "solution" was to soldier on without a plan, take her to the barbecue and just hope for the best. He said nothing about the factory gossip … he just hoped she wouldn't get wind of it and the blokes would behave. It wasn't the most watertight of plans, he had to admit.

About 20 people turned up on the day, which was sunny but had an autumnal chill in the air. Miraculously, Sean got away with it. Tracey was magnificent. For a start, she looked fantastic in a bottle-green dress (respectably short), which she'd bought specially, but, best of all, she blended in smoothly and said all the right things. Two or three of them recognised her from the café and gave Sean a hard time about having kept the local connection a secret. Tracey knew that he hadn't said anything at work about her café, and didn't mind — in fact, she was glad not to have his work colleagues coming in to scrutinise her — but she joined in the ribbing of her boyfriend by complaining loudly that he was bad for business because he'd not told anyone about how good her coffee was. That went down well and made her "one of the boys".

Sean was impressed at the way, without the safety of her café counter, she confidently chatted to his workmates, most of whom were complete strangers to her, and said all the right things. She was at ease talking about the footy, reality TV programs and work, and there was not a hint of anything even slightly religious. She did girly chat with the other women and transformed into one of the blokes when necessary. When one of the apprentices told a dirty joke to a group of men and one or two women, Tracey laughed even though Sean would never dare tell her a joke like that. When another of his workmates — who, by then, had had a few beers — made an unsubtle allusion to Sean and Tracey's supposed nocturnal habits, she deflected him with ease. "You don't know the half of it," she joked without skipping a beat.

Despite her success with his workmates, she admitted afterwards that she had been quite nervous and found the whole thing very stressful. The admission surprised Sean because she had seemed very much at ease with everyone, but he was quietly pleased that she did occasionally doubt herself and struggled to put on a confident air. After all, it had been a struggle for him in this relationship to try and rise to her standards.

Tracey did talk religion with someone at the barbecue though. Away from the main group in the kitchen after they'd eaten, she fell in with the boss's wife, Joanne. She was older — late 30s, Tracey guessed — and Joanne asked Tracey why she was drinking nothing stronger than fruit juice. When one of Sean's colleagues had questioned her about this earlier, she'd deflected him by making a joke: "Gosh, you wouldn't want to see me drink anything stronger. I'd be a train wreck." This time with Joanne she chose to explain why she wasn't drinking alcohol because she'd noticed that Joanne wasn't drinking either.

"It's because of my religion," she said, volunteering nothing further.

Joanne, however, was curious. "Really? That's interesting. That's the same reason I don't drink. Well, not often."

"What religion are you?"

"Adventist. And you?"

"Bahá'í"

Joanne hadn't heard that word before and she asked Tracey to repeat it.

"A lot of people have trouble pronouncing it at first," said Tracey. "Tell me about Bar-hi."

And Tracey did. She also asked why Joanne was an Adventist and what she believed, and whether her husband was of the same religion. He wasn't interested in religion, she found out. Tracey wanted to ask whether this was a problem but now wasn't the time to pursue that point, she decided. Still, they did have an excellent 20-minute conversation inside while Sean was outside with the guys talking footy.

"Bloody oath, mate, that Tracey's one hot chick," Gazza, a cabinet installer, told him. Gazza had been as crude as anyone at work about her, and Sean braced for what would come next but it was better than he expected. "I don't get how you managed to land a chick like that, with your big nose, fat bum and short legs! Has she got a sister?"

"Mate, it's my all-round charm and charisma that did the trick," Sean replied.

Basking in the glow of Tracey's outstanding performance in front of his workmates, Sean went off in search of her, finding her in the kitchen with the boss's wife. As she saw Sean approaching, Tracey seamlessly broke off from what she was saying — about how she respected Jesus but believed He had returned in the form of her faith's prophet, Bahá'u'lláh — and said: "So, Mr O'Riordan, what have you been up to out there?"

"Oh, doing an in-depth analysis of this season's footy prospects," he said as he put his arm around Tracey. "And what's on the agenda out here?"

Joanne answered first. "Discussing whether there's life after footy."

They all laughed. Tracey was impressed by Joanne, but not as much as Sean was impressed by Tracey. So impressed that he decided that night he would actually go to a Bahá'í meeting and find out about her faith. Tracey's barbecue performance earned her lots of brownie points. Enough, a romantic might say, to suggest that he was falling in love with her. She made all the other women there that afternoon look second-rate by comparison. Tracey was like a footballer leaping above everyone to take a mark. But he knew that if their relationship was to progress further, he needed to take some interest in her religion.

They went to a meeting and Sean was surprised to find the talk was more logical than he had expected. The other Bahá'ís were even relatively normal — not the religious zombies he'd feared. In fact, there was a rather beautiful Iranian girl ... no, he mustn't start coveting other women. As Sean became increasingly more open to religious discussion, one night over a curry he raised the subject of God and how he couldn't be sure that God existed.

"Well, I can't prove anything. You just have to have faith," Tracey told him.

"Logically, your religion makes sense but it doesn't land the killer knockout punch that proves God is the heavyweight champion of the universe," he said, raising his fists and feigning a boxing pose.

"Logic is all about the head and the brain. Men go there first and sometimes never get beyond that area."

"What do you mean? I thought women usually accused men of only being interested in one thing — something that's much lower down the body!"

Tracey was on a roll and was unfazed by this crude reference. "It's all similar. The world of logic is all about physical reality and sexual gratification is very much just a physical thing."

"How do you know that?" Sean asked provocatively, fully aware that Tracey had never had sex.

"It's what friends tell me," she replied without any sign of defensiveness. "It's not love. There's no lasting depth to sex without love."

"I'm a friend and I don't think sex is a purely physical thing."

Tracey wanted to get back to the point she had been trying to make.

"Look, I was talking about logic and how men want things to be proved logically. Believing in God requires more than that. You have to be lifted to a higher plane, to experience God without the use of your five senses."

Sean paused to think about that.

"So how do I get to that higher plane?"

"Well, that's why we have Manifestations, or Prophets, of God. They are how we find God. Baha'u'lláh is that means for this age."

"But He lived two centuries ago in a part of the world that is nothing like the world I know."

"When you know the story of His life, the ordeals He went through, the sacrifices, the way He never wavered, His teachings about the purpose of life, the love He had for everyone — you can't help but feel a power in Him that is totally unique. It's a pure love like no other form of love. How can this not be God talking through Him to humanity?"

Sean felt like Tracey herself had just risen to a higher plane of intensity. "I could never be religious enough to hear God talking to me," he said, now much more serious than he had just been. "You could try teaching me but I'd be a lousy student."

"I love a challenge. I so want to be your teacher!"

Her smile was the biggest he had ever seen and he knew resistance was futile. From then, almost every time they saw each other, they would talk about God, Baha'u'lláh, religion and the search for the higher plane. Tracey prayed for him every day. Intensely.

As is normal when a relationship blossoms into a thousand colours, this one took over Sean and Tracey's lives, but then, four months later, Tracey suffered a blow that became an even greater preoccupation. Without warning, her mother was diagnosed with advanced ovarian cancer and given about six months to live. Tracey was very close to her mother who had raised her and her older brother, Gavin, as a single parent since the children's father walked out just after Tracey turned six. Her mum never remarried, never went out with another man. She devoted herself to raising the two children.

The day Tracey heard the news it devastated her. Sean took the afternoon off work to be with her and her mum. Tracey was drowning in tears. Her mother hugged her and tried without success to calm her when, logically, it should have been Tracey comforting her mother. It was like a funeral, only no one had died. At least, not yet. Sean had never been this close to such depth of pain and emotion, and open expression of it. He didn't know how to handle it or what to say, other than just to be there for them. If anything, his greatest concern was for Tracey, who had gone into a complete meltdown. He'd never seen even a hint of such raw emotion from her; she was always so controlled.

The next day Sean and Tracey rang and texted each other numerous times and although she sounded fragile, she seemed to have got herself back under control.

"Mum's going to die," she told Sean. "I have to accept that and help her make the journey to the next world. She has a shaky belief in God and she's frightened." She even managed a small joke. "Gee, I'm surrounded by shaky souls!"

Day by day, Sean observed Tracey at work on her mission. It was amazing to see. She was utterly devoted to comforting her mother in her encounter with death and did it with an unspoken love that he could hear as clearly as if she were shouting it. Her mother's illness and spiritual journey took precedence over everything else in Tracey's life. The café takings fell because she was hardly there;

she slept most nights at her mum's and time with Sean was strictly rationed, although she could never apologise enough to him for this. One evening when he left her to go home, she held him tight and whispered, "Thank you ... for everything," and kissed him full on the lips. True to the no-sex rule, they had never made love and physical contact had only briefly, that once, gone beyond pecks on the cheek, holding hands or walking arm-in-arm. So a kiss like this had a new potency. Sean wondered if there was a message in that kiss or whether it was just about the emotion surrounding her mother's illness. Meanwhile, Tracey was wondering too. She had done it without thinking and had never kissed anyone like that before. Was the kiss about her mum or about Sean?

Despite her storm of conflicting emotions, Tracey started seriously contemplating if she could give her mother the most wonderful of gifts before she died: her daughter's marriage. She and Sean had grown really close and he was being fantastically supportive during the illness. She had been quite brutal about religion and sex that first night she went out with him and it hadn't deterred him, as it had previous boys. His total lack of interest in religion at the beginning had dissolved and he was now going to Bahá'í meetings and he was even in the 5th week of a Bahá'í study circle. But she didn't know yet where this journey would take him; how deep would he go with religion or was he just showing interest for her sake? Maybe it was too soon to make the call, but if he got to her prescribed destination, that "higher plane", a short time after her mother died, it would be almost unbearable to marry without her mum being there. If she tried to fast-track him into marriage, her motive might be all wrong. Or did she have enough faith to know that he was a good man and would get there one day, maybe not this year, maybe not next year, but eventually? She prayed hard for him.

Then about three months after her mother's diagnosis, Sean became a Bahá'í by signing an enrolment card that said he accepted the Bahá'í Faith. He did it secretly, Tracey didn't know, and he staged the breaking of the news. He took time off work one afternoon and went to the café, where he knew she was working that day and would be preparing to close. He got a long black and drank it at the counter, talking to her as she cleaned up. He was the last customer of the day.

When he had finished and she was ready to lock up, he reached into his pocket for his wallet. She thought he was going to pay and quickly intercepted the attempt: "Don't be silly. It's on the house."

"No, I think you'll want what I've got in here."

He pulled out his completed Bahá'í enrolment card, which she'd given him a few weeks earlier. He placed it on the counter in front of Tracey with an exaggerated flourish. It took Tracey completely by surprise. She came round the counter, jumped at Sean and locked her arms and legs around him with vice-like grip. This was something else she had never done before.

"I had no idea you were even close to becoming a Bahá'í," she said, her eyes brimming with tears.

"It just goes to show that no matter how well you think you know someone, you don't know them as well as you thought."

He made the comment jokingly but it tormented Tracey over the next few days. Although the card had been a fabulous surprise, she worried about how genuine his motive was. Might there be other less pleasant surprises? Did she truly know him? She could spend years trying to flush out what lay hidden in Sean's dark recesses and it may all be in vain.

She questioned Sean persistently about his decision to become a Bahá'í. She wanted to reassure herself that he had done it for the right reasons. She didn't want either of them to be blinded by emotions. He answered all her questions convincingly but she couldn't bring herself to ask the critical question: had he enrolled for himself or for her?

Instead, someone else asked him: his sister, Danni. She had a way of lighting his touch paper like no one else with her provocative bluntness. His big sister was his childhood persecutor and continued to bait him as an adult.

"Listen, Sean. It's your business but this is me, your older and wiser sister, speaking. Do you really — I mean, r-e-a-l-l-y! — accept everything this bloody religion says or are you just desperate to rush her down the aisle and into bed?"

"You're right. It's my business, not yours."

"Oh, come on, answer me."

"Like you would have answered me if I'd stuck my nose into your business and asked you whether you knew what you were doing when you started going out with that loser, that career crook, who's now your ex-husband?"

"Piss off. Like you've never screwed up!"

From there, the argument only escalated, with personal insults freely traded, and Sean never answered her question … but afterwards he did give a lot more than passing thought to what his answer might have been.

A week later, Tracey sat in her flat with Sean and asked another question: "Tell me something, Sean O'Riordan. How do you feel about me?"

"How do I feel?"

"How do you feel … about me?"

"Isn't it obvious I'm crazy about you, babe?"

"You make it sound like a mental condition."

"Eh?"

"Do you think we'll stay together … forever?"

She was really asking him if he would marry her.

"I hope so." He shifted uncomfortably.

"That's what I think too."

"Oh."

"So, what shall we do about it then?"

Now he realised where this was going. "I think I should ask you to marry me," he said.

Just over a month later, almost a year since Sean had first stepped into the café, Tracey was sitting on her sofa stroking her cat, Tabatha. She had just closed the book she was reading and placed it on the floor. Sean was by her side, flicking through a magazine. They were a week away from getting married and the hastily planned wedding — so her mother could be there to witness it — was an unstoppable force. Plane tickets had been booked. All over the country, all over the world, friends and relatives were packing their bags to come. An army of caterers was briefed and ready to prepare the feast.

There was a lot to worry about and tonight, although the couple were sitting side by side on the sofa supposedly reading, their thoughts were elsewhere. Sean was worrying about his wedding speech. His family, especially his ex-brother-in-law, was an easy target for jokes he might never get away with at any other time, but should he keep his speech joke-free out of respect for Tracey's mum? Tracey was worrying about eternity.

Maybe it was just pre-marriage nerves, Tracey thought. Like everyone has, right? But, for her, a marriage commitment meant forever and the enormity of that was troubling her. This wasn't like buying something in a shop — keep the receipt and take it back if you change your mind. She was investing too much in this commitment to be casual about it. She worried that, in her excitement at finding Sean and her distress over her mother's cancer, she wasn't thinking straight.

She knew Sean had been fantastic to her. Gentle, respectful, kind and loving. She'd never experienced all of this in one man, but there were differences between them. For one thing, he'd slept with other girls; she had had no sexual experience. He'd become a Bahá'í but did he really accept the Faith as fully as she did? Had he truly accepted for himself Bahá'u'lláh's claim about who He was or had he done it more to please her? Was he as fully committed as she was to the idea of marriage being forever? It was much easier to agree to marriage when you didn't factor in the troubling thought that this would be forever, throughout all the worlds of God, not just until the novelty wore off or until someone younger and sexier came along. Maybe it was all about the intensity of belief in God. Tracey thought about God and saw God in all sorts of places throughout every day. She prayed first thing in the morning, at midday and last thing at night — they were priorities, around which everything else fitted. She tried to get Sean to do the same but he said he didn't feel comfortable praying — too many memories from childhood of hypocritical piety.

If God was constantly at the forefront of her mind, how would she cope with a husband who maybe rarely thought about God but treated footy players as gods? And who didn't have the same sort of commitment that she had? Perhaps she was underestimating him but maybe this was how it would always be. If they'd not been in such a rush to get married before she lost her mother, would they have eventually broken off their engagement?

Oblivious to Tabatha purring contentedly in her lap, she was agonising over major spiritual matters whereas she guessed he was probably thinking about what sex with her would be like. But then Tracey had thought about sex as well: she had no idea what he would be like in bed. Maybe he'd want to do things that she didn't. He may have got some fancy ideas from watching internet porn. They might be sexually incompatible. Maybe she'd be a disappointment to him after his sexual adventures with other girls, who were also perhaps graduates of internet porn studies. They hadn't discussed any of this and it was one more thing to worry about, albeit an earthier kind of worry.

There was something else too: age. She was 31, he was 25. Tracey understood that girls matured much faster than boys. Some boys never matured! Never got past their obsession with sex, footy and cars. He may be a long way behind her in terms of maturity. Maybe commitment to marriage, to God and to religion came more readily with a maturity he had not yet attained. And maybe never would. Her mother had quizzed her about the age gap: was it a problem? Tracey had insisted there was no problem. Now she wasn't so sure.

Still stroking Tabatha, she turned to Sean and, almost as if talking to herself, asked: "You do know this marriage is forever, don't you?"

Sean was immersed in thinking through a joke he wanted to tell as part of his wedding speech. It was about his sister's husband and required careful framing. "What?"

"I just want to make sure about something important. For me, marriage is a commitment for eternity. Through all the worlds of God, forever, we'll be one. Do you see marriage like that?"

Sean looked slightly bemused. "Yeah, of course."

"I mean, forever is a long time to hang around someone if you go off them."

"What?"

"Once the novelty of sex has worn off, I mean, will you still love me? Will you still love me when I'm 64 and frumpy?"

"Don't be stupid. Of course I will, Trace. And anyway, you'll never be frumpy. What's all this about?"

Tracey paused and took a deep breath, still stroking the cat, but her eyes drilled like laser beams into his face. "I just want to make sure, you know. That's all. It's a big commitment. Forever's a long time, after all."

Where was that fun, relaxed girl he met in the café? And that's when he said it, a weak kind of joke. "Forever? I thought it was only until death do us part." Tracey stared hard at Sean. She wasn't laughing.

"Suppose in a year or two, some hottie in a short skirt comes on to you?"

"Now you're being paranoid."

"Suppose! And you go out for a drink with her and she makes it plain that she's up for a bit of fun. Wife needn't know. No commitment. Would you — "

"Stop it, Trace!"

"Would you invent a reason for going out after work one night and then going back to her place? Would you?"

"Enough!"

"Because if you're not in this forever, the offer might be hard to resist. After all, we might have a kid by then. Sleep might be all I want at night. Miss Come-Up-And-See-Me-Sometime might be too tempting to resist."

"I don't see why we need to talk about this, Trace. This is ridiculous. Are you accusing me of not being serious about our marriage? Because you're starting to sound like my mother and my sister, and they're ball-breakers."

Sean got up and headed for the kitchen, pretending he wanted a drink. Tracey stared into empty space, regretting what she had just said.

"I'm sorry," she called out.

A week later Tracey and Sean stood in front of 150 family and friends, and, most importantly, in front of Tracey's mum, and said the Bahá'í wedding vow: "Verily, I abide by the will of God." And they committed themselves to eternity. Sean's sister committed herself fully to the celebrations and, slurring her words as she leaned heavily on Sean's shoulder, made a point of telling them both: "Youse two make a great couple."

Tracey and Sean had a one-night honeymoon at a local hotel. By now, Tracey's mum was too ill for them to feel that they could go away. A week later, with Tracey, her brother and his wife and Sean at her bedside, she slipped away. They all said through their tears that the wedding had helped her to die more comfortably.

"Besides, she's not gone," Tracey said. "She'll be with us all forever."

Sean tried to imagine what forever would be like, leaving their bodies behind and travelling together throughout eternity. He couldn't do it, not now. His head was flooded with the emotions of the past week.

Tracey looked across at him and smiled gently.

BLONDE BOMBSHELL

No matter how much kindliness ye may
expend upon the liar, he will but lie the more,
for he believeth you to be deceived, while
ye understand him but too well, and only
remain silent out of your extreme compassion.
— 'Abdul-Bahá, Selections from the Writings

"MEET ME AT The Vic after work at 6 on Friday." That was
the instruction. No "Is this convenient for you?" or any identifying
features like "I'll be wearing a red jacket, reading the new Liane
Moriarty novel." Well, that's the sort of book he imagined a girl on
a dating app might read. He had seen one or two young women in
Dymocks looking at one of her books in the bestsellers section —
not rigorous research but sufficient evidence for this sort of project.
Ideally, he would like a girl to be reading a classic. Maybe Jane
Austen or George Eliot. Or, better still but most unlikely, something scientific. But that was wishful thinking. He had lowered his
expectations since turning 30; lowered himself to a dating app. All

he had was the photo of her from the dating app and a brief description. Her name was Pip. She was blonde and aged 25. A teacher and "gym junkie" who read a lot — no mention of favourite authors. To his relief, she'd also written: "No ONS". This made it clear that she wasn't using the app for one-night stands. Hopefully, that wasn't a lie. He, too, wasn't on the app for sex. He believed in friendship first, sex later. With friendship as his initial goal, he had wanted to find out more about her before they met — some research before meeting face to face — but she had shut down that idea abruptly. Despite that, he had decided to take the risk of going ahead and meeting her anyway. Well, she was the first girl to respond positively to him on the app and the list of rejections had been long.

He had Pip's photo on his mobile and, hiding it close to his midriff in both hands as he walked from his office through the fading autumn sunshine to the pub, he kept glancing down at her as if to make sure that she was still there. It was a rather murky photo but she certainly looked beautiful and had a nice smile in which he sensed some vulnerability. That suspicion of vulnerability interested him. All the same, he knew that dating app photos were notoriously deceptive and possibly not even of the person they purported to be. "Slim and sexy" could often turn out to be "fat and flabby"; "25" could be "35". Then he remembered that he had lied about his own age, slicing off four years and putting him on the right side of 30. His photo, too, was not very recent but at least his black hair hadn't changed. It was still the same "respectable" (his mother's term) length and lifelong style; nor had the hairline retreated. Revealing his mother's Chinese heritage in a photo, however, always made him nervous. He attributed his lack of any other matches on the app to his Asian features. Or was he being paranoid? Whether or not he was, Pip being his first and only match convinced him to "carpe diem" (his academic father's expression).

It felt as if the pub exploded in his face when he opened the heavy door and entered the Vic. It was the noise he struggled to absorb: conversation-crushing music blared out and everyone seemed to be shouting. A group of three young men in T-shirts were loudly goading each other at one table. A couple of big groups of workmates were laughing loudly around other tables crammed prematurely for this time of night with empty bottles and glasses. Animated conversations at yet more tables seemed to be in competition with each other. It was a typical Friday night as workers' weekday discipline was thrown to the weekend wind. "No way was I having that … " "They've got no chance, mate … " "Did you see the look she gave him? …" "They do curries to die for … " "Didn't you know his brother's in prison? … " It all heightened his anxiety. This wasn't familiar territory. How was he going to be able to hold a conversation with someone he'd never met before in all this noise? Why did she want to meet in this wholly unsuitable place? He really should have seized the initiative and chosen the meeting place. A quiet restaurant perhaps. The dim lighting was the only source of comfort he could find, but he tried to look confident.

Most of the people in the pub were like him — his age and younger. Well, not completely like him because he was probably the only man there looking for a blonde he had "met" on an app. He had been here before with work colleagues but on quieter nights than this. (A Queen song was now crashing over everyone.) It had a log fire in the main bar and dark décor only slightly illuminated by the low lighting. It felt old in a reliable kind of way. The many framed photos of long-gone city buildings and old footy players added to the feeling of age.

The subdued lighting made it hard to scan the crowd for the blonde gym junkie. He was standing near the entry door. Some people were hidden from view behind other heads or had their backs to him. It felt like they'd positioned themselves deliberately to get in his way. He spotted a blonde on a far table. He had to crane his neck to get a clear view but he wanted to do so in a discreet way that didn't draw attention to himself. He was taking no chances and so it was an exhaustive and slow process. He had slipped his phone into his jacket pocket when he first entered, thinking it would help him look relaxed rather than nervous. Now he withdrew it and studied the photo against the real thing facing his direction at the distant table. The hair was the right length and there were no facial features at odds with the photo. Just when he was satisfied that this was the evasive Pip sitting alone at the table, an older woman approached her. They embraced and sat back down together. Maybe they were mother and daughter, but clearly this wasn't Pip because a girl doesn't bring her mother on a date. Back to the drawing board. He sighed again, then, looking forlornly at the photo, he smiled at his predicament and said under his breath with a touch of black humour: "This is really giving me the pip!"

He looked at his watch. It was now five past six. He'd been early but now he was late. Although there were other blondes in the bar, none of them were alone. Surely she wouldn't have arranged a date at a place where she would be among her friends? He moved to a different vantage point beside the door to the toilets — not the most comfortable of locations — but still it yielded no other Pip possibilities.

It was now 10 past and he was ready to give up. He moved to the end of the bar and got out his mobile phone — if it made him look nervous, well, he was nervous. Anyway, he reasoned, people are constantly on their mobiles these days so it would be viewed as nothing unusual. Pip didn't have his number but she may have sent a message to the dating app. As he fumbled his way into the app, he took yet another quick glance at the crowd and there, just entering the pub and heading his way, was an unaccompanied blonde.

She appeared slightly agitated, even looking about her as if searching for someone. This had to be her, now just three or four metres away with one arm on the bar and standing with her back to him. She was still studying the crowd, probably worrying that she was late and looking for him. The one direction in which she hadn't looked was his. Strange how often we see everything and everyone except that which is closest to us, he thought. He remembered how his mother would respond when someone — always him or his father — couldn't find something and, pointing it out inches away from where they were standing, she would say: "It's there, you silly thing, looking at you." Well, now he was sure it was Pip looking for him but not finding him … and he was in his mother's role of seeing what she couldn't see.

He moved towards her but she was still looking away. "Excuse me, I'm Christopher," he said in a quiet voice drowned out by Michael Jackson's Beat It and the sound of 100 people all shouting to each other at once. It was no surprise she didn't hear him and remained with her back to him. Even having lowered his voice, he felt people turning towards him and preparing to rescue the girl from this pervert. But far from being heard by half the pub, it seemed no one heard a thing, including Pip herself. Despite that, he was standing so close to her that he could smell her perfume. He had already moved in close in a failed attempt to make sure she could hear him and others couldn't. It was pervert proximity and he self-consciously took a step backwards. As he did so, she turned in his direction and was taken aback to find him up uncomfortably close to her. She, too, backed away and the look on her face showed her clear annoyance at this unwelcome approach.

"I'm sorry," he said in a louder voice, anxious to retrieve the situation and to make a smoother landing. "Are you Pip? Christopher — um, that's me. From the dating app?"

This time she heard and the annoyance turned to something less hostile — was it puzzlement, thoughtfulness or relief, he wondered? He noticed two other people at the bar had heard him and were looking at him intimidatingly. He hated that he had been reduced to finding a girlfriend this way and having to accost young women in public places.

Slowly, a smile spread across her face. "God, it's a good job you knew my name from the dating app. I'd be a bit suspicious otherwise."

"Yes, I'm sorry. I'm a novice at this sort of thing and I haven't mastered the art of the opening line."

"That's OK. At least you've turned up. So, Christopher, it's good to meet you. Let's go have a drink. There's an empty table over there. I'll go grab it if you can get me a red wine." She patted him on one of his hands which was clenched tight. She had taken the initiative and was already heading to the table — without apologising for being late — before he had even had a chance to realise that he had failed miserably to assert himself. Again.

As Christopher waited to order, he sneaked a look at Pip. He felt pleased with himself because she was pretty enough to catch any man's eye, as she had been on the app, though, on reflection, she didn't seem as close a match to her photo as he had thought when he first noticed her. For one thing, her hair was much shorter but women are always changing their hairstyle. She had removed her coat and was wearing a loose turquoise shirt and black skirt. It wasn't exactly an adventurous dress sense. At least they had that in common. As he watched her, he noticed that she was still looking around, mostly towards the door. Was she looking for someone? He was puzzled.

Joining her at the table, having precariously navigated his way through the crowd with their two drinks, he asked if she wanted something to eat. Pip couldn't hear what he was saying and got him to repeat the question in a louder voice.

"No thanks, Chris," she said, drilling her voice through the din like a projectile. He hated having his name shortened but he didn't say anything. "I've already eaten too much today and I've got to watch the calories." Not that she looked to Christopher as if she was anywhere close to having a weight problem.

He had bought himself a black coffee because it seemed the best way to keep a clear head and Pip was quick to seize on this unusual choice of drink in a Friday night pub.

"So nothing stronger than coffee for you? That's interesting. A man's choice of drink says a lot about him." He explained that he didn't drink beer and didn't feel like anything stronger than coffee. "OK," she said, with what he took as an implication that there was something naff about drinking coffee in a pub. An early black mark.

The feathery touch of her hand at the bar had given him a slight shudder. This was ridiculous, he thought. He may be 32 (28 as far as Pip knew), have a doctorate and work for a mining company, but tonight he felt like a teenager trying to pick up a girl for the first time. The touch reminded him of clumsy teenage fumblings and that embarrassing time in Year 12 when a Year 10 girl had flirted with him. It also reminded him that he had no idea who this Pip really was and what she really wanted — casual chat or casual sex? Maybe her real goal was to fast-track them into bed, despite her stated "no ONS"? Was the touch of her hand some sort of sign? He floundered with mating rituals. He was the bookworm forced into playing AFL footy and hopelessly out of his depth.

Pip moved on from her interest in his coffee by asking where he worked. She was impressed by his doctorate and asked him what his work involved. This was comfortable terrain for Christopher. He spoke in some detail about how he was able to work remotely at mine sites without leaving his city office and how it was possible to do this. She presented an interested face.

After a while, he realised that he had said too much and he stopped abruptly. "So, have you been doing this for long?" he asked.

"Using dating apps? On and off. When I feel the need. I've met some strange guys."

Christopher shuffled uneasily in his wobbly wooden chair. "Hopefully not tonight though," he said.

Pip scrutinised him with a look that seemed to say: "I'm not sure about that." But all she actually said was: "You're doing OK so far." She was quite intimidating.

"Who's been the worst of these guys?"

"Most of them have been losers with no idea about how to talk to a girl. They talk about themselves, ask nothing about me and have got just one thing on their minds."

"Oh," Christopher said self-consciously. "I suppose that's why you said you didn't do one-night stands. Well, nor do I.

"So you don't find me attractive then?" she grinned. Christopher struggled to find an adequate answer but Pip let him off the hook. "It's OK, you don't have to answer that."

The conversation moved on to their families, Pip's job — she was a primary school teacher being given a hard time by her principal — and their interests. Pip was into English soccer (her team was Chelsea) and AFL (the Bombers); watched a lot of crime and reality TV shows; was addicted to Instagram and read magazines rather than books. Christopher didn't follow any sport, only ever watched the news and documentaries, hated social media, spent most of his time on the computer researching and was always reading two or three books at any one time, none of them easy reads.

Despite this, they both managed to find something in each other's interests that sustained conversation — Christopher knew about the drug scandal at the Bombers and Pip showed interest in the looming federal election. It took a while to find shared interests, but eventually some emerged. They both liked movies, but different types. Christopher's all-time favourite was The Shawshank Redemption; Pip nominated Slumdog Millionaire. They both liked Indian curries and swimming and they both had dogs. They both went to a gym and both had had sessions with chiropractors.

As the conversation started to flow more easily, Christopher started to adjust to the noise and to Pip, and to relax more.

"How about we go to a couple of movies — one that you choose and one that I choose — and see if we can learn to like something we wouldn't otherwise have gone to see?" Christopher said with growing confidence.

"Or, if we just can't agree on films or TV programs, we can talk about our aches and pains, chiropractors we have hated and how gorgeous our dogs are," Pip joked.

She looked at her watch. "Oh my God, it's almost 7 o'clock," she said. "I must go."

The sudden end to the evening after less than 50 minutes took Christopher by surprise. He had expected the conversation to develop into a meal at a restaurant. "Right, I see," he said, suddenly deflated and failing to hide it. "Um, are you sure you don't want another drink?"

"Oh, no," she laughed. "I won't be able to sleep if I have any more wine." Then, without any noticeable pause, she continued: "Now, tell me, have I passed the test? Shall we do the movies sometime? And were you just pretending when you said you didn't do one-night stands?"

Christopher was unprepared for such blunt questions. He tried to avoid answering the last question. "It's not a test, Pip, just a conversation, and I've enjoyed talking to you. I — "

"Look, it's OK. If I'm not your type, it's OK. Just be honest with me."

"I was going to say I'd like to see a movie with you. You choose which one. I'd really like that."

Pip smiled to herself but didn't say anything.

"Are you lost for words?"

"Kind of. It's just that you've surprised me by not being all that interested in sex — that's mainly what most blokes want — and you suggested going to see my kind of movie, as opposed to your kind of movie. Men will go to great lengths to avoid chick flicks."

Now he was lost for words.

Pip picked up her empty glass and rubbed an index finger round the rim, surely pondering more than just the shape of the glass.

"Before we go any further, if there is any further, you need to know something." She stared at the glass. "I'm not Pip." She paused, expecting an angry response, but got none. So she pressed on. "You asked me if I was Pip, you seemed like a nice guy and so I pretended to be the girl from your dating app. You let slip that your Pip was a teacher so I made out to be a teacher too. But I'm not. Sorry. I've deceived you and cheated the real Pip out of her date. I did it on the spur of the moment and it was wrong. I'm sorry."

Christopher couldn't look at her. Gazing at the wooden table, he asked: "What's your real name then?"

"Amber. Amber the dental nurse. Look, it's been nice meeting you but I'll go now. Have a good life. Go make it up to Pip. Sorry."

As she rose to leave, Christopher looked up at her and spoke slowly. "If we stick to the movie plan, will there be any more 'Pip' moments? Will you lie again?"

Amber avoided eye contact and stared at the door. "Not if you let me be me," she said cautiously. "Not if I don't have to pretend any more to be someone I'm not." Christopher tried to unpick these cryptic clues but didn't say anything. Amber sat down again. Now she looked at him. "If I don't like your movie, I want to be able to tell you so and it's OK if you don't like my choice either. No hurt feelings, eh?"

Christopher leaned forward, elbows on the table, hands clasped together and propping up his chin. She dipped conspiratorially forward as well, placing her hands on the table and almost touching him.

"Well, OK, then, truth test: do you actually want to see me again?" he asked. "Be honest."

She thought about her answer before replying: "Yes, you're kinda cute but you need to loosen up, and, actually, I think you need a girl like me. I could be good for you. Honestly."

THERE, BUT NOT FULLY

> *… man should know his own self*
> *and recognise that which leadeth unto*
> *loftiness or lowliness, glory or abasement,*
> *wealth or poverty.*
>
> — Bahá'u'lláh, Tablets of Bahá'u'lláh

FIVE TO EIGHT and he's starting his usual morning ritual of driving to work. He's on a kind of automatic pilot. Turn right, right again, then left, now he's approaching the traffic lights at the main road. They're red and he glides slowly to a halt behind the queue of cars. He looks approvingly at the flat tummies and leotarded legs of the yummy mummies bounding out of a session at the upmarket yoga centre; he imagines himself back on Lygon Street in Melbourne inhaling the tempting Bolognese aroma that will be wafting later from the Italian restaurant next-door to the centre. But then, suddenly, he remembers. The back door! Did he close it? He was the last one to leave the house. His wife had left for work an hour earlier. His mind is blank. He has no recollection of it at all. He had opened all the doors first thing to cool the house before the onslaught of summer heat later in the day and also to let the smell of the jasmine on the back fence sweeten the stale smell of last night's stir-fry. But did he forget to close the back door? He remembers closing the study door — he'd paused to inhale the heady scent of the jasmine — and, naturally, he closed the front door behind him when he left. But the back door in the kitchen …

This has happened before. It's like an irritating itch. Sometimes, after driving down his street, he has been unable to resist the temptation of going back and making sure he closed a door. And each time it has proved unnecessary. He has indeed closed, and locked, the door. The locked door always stares dumbfounded at him, as if to say how could he possibly not remember?

It's just forgetfulness, nothing more serious, though it's worried him enough to turn to the all-powerful God, Google, and check out whether it's really as normal and harmless as he's chosen to believe. After all, he can't possibly be going senile. That's a problem only for older people who've reached 60 or 70 or whenever old age officially starts. He's only early 40s, for goodness' sake. All the same, he wishes these little memory lapses didn't bother him so much.

He takes comfort in a theory, which he compiled without the gravitas of a Master's degree or doctorate, without scientific analysis of a study group and without any research funding. Indeed, without any scientific rigour at all; just an observation really, although "theory" makes it sound more substantial. The theory goes like this: we live parts of our life without being fully or even slightly present. Closing and locking doors before we go out is one of those automatic processes, done without any thought and, therefore, often not remembered. It's not that other more important matters are weighing heavily on his mind at the time; in fact, he's almost certain that he wasn't thinking about anything in particular at the time he left his house a couple of minutes ago. Unlike now, as he sits at the traffic lights, suddenly whisked away from Lygon Street restaurants and consumed by thoughts of that back door. And it's almost certain that when these traffic lights turn green, he will turn back home to check whether he actually did lock that door. He is trying to take the sting out of his frustration by imagining himself as a blank canvas awaiting artistic inspiration. Well, it sounds good but the only thing he sees on that canvas is an open door and the frustration persists.

Sitting later in the café where he always goes at lunchtime — just across the road from his office — he returns to his traffic light ruminations as he drinks from a can of Coke Zero. He's been on automatic pilot plenty of times. The daily drive to work; opening the fridge. He does such routine activities robotically or at least without much conscious engagement. He can't remember anything specific about nearly all his many morning drives to work, apart from that time someone ran into the back of his car. That was a reality crash-landing. And he's embarrassed to admit how frequently he arrives at the fridge or a cupboard or even a room and can't remember for a few moments why he's gone there — but everyone does that, don't they?

OK, so if those sorts of things are routine and don't warrant deep engagement, even driving without being fully present, do we also zone out when dealing with really important matters, he ponders over his lunchtime wrap? Blindsided by something really important and obvious that we never saw coming? Blindsided because we weren't paying close enough attention? Preoccupied with something trivial and not noticing the big snake slithering towards us? Too busy taking a selfie.

He's thinking of major events in life; those big intersections that weren't marked on the map. Marriage breakup. Loss of religious belief. Serious illness. Drug addiction. Financial disaster. Career cul-de-sac. Loss of friendship. Family estrangement. Loneliness. Those sorts of things.

Marriage breakup is something with which he is all too familiar. He didn't go into marriage expecting it to fail but now he knows he went into it without giving much thought to long-term compatibility. It was the sex. With the wisdom of hindsight, it seems stupid but at the time he was obsessed with it; now though he sees that his ex-wife's much greater sexual experience was a warning sign. If he'd realised that then, he would have worked out that she probably wasn't the full "till-death-us-do-part" type. If he had talked to a counsellor, preferably a man because a man would have better understood him, the counsellor would have said that he was blinded by love or, rather, something he mistook for love. It was like one of those horrible online scams where some poisonous persuader talks a lonely heart into parting with their life savings for a promise of the love they crave and, of course, they are blinded. They've failed to see the danger signs. Anyway, that's what he blames for his divorce after five years of marriage. Not that he ever craved love or paid a high price for the failure of the marriage. No, he wasn't desperate or destroyed. Definitely not.

He didn't buy his ex-wife's version of what went wrong. She accused him of changing from a funny and committed lover into a "sullen killjoy". Those two words are branded indelibly in his memory — no danger of him ever forgetting them — and he bristles whenever he thinks of them. As a so-called "sullen killjoy", he became "obsessed" about their financial situation, according to her. He apparently used it to say no to holidays and much-needed things like a new car and air-conditioning. Even now, 12 years on from the divorce, he hasn't softened his resistance to these accusations. Just as she vehemently rejected his accusation that she was seeing another man; only that was the truth.

As he drinks from his can of Coke (a drink his current wife doesn't approve of), he does wonder if they couldn't both have foreseen their difficulties before they leapt out of bed into marriage.

Now he is convinced that she was even seeing someone else in-between their nightly romps before they married, but he was misty-eyed with lust and missed the signs.

His parents, after about 30 years of marriage, suggested he wait longer before he married "this girl", two words that his father said so disparagingly. His sister certainly heeded their advice. She went out with her future husband for six years and then was engaged to him for three more before they finally walked down the aisle. But he didn't have his sister's patience. He was young and naïve and his parents' caution seemed pointlessly obstructive. Anyway, when you're young, why apply the brake? Life is for living, ready or not. Probably, they saw "this girl" as wanting to whisk away their only son and spend all his money. Maybe in his parents' day it was normal for couples to take longer before making the marriage commitment, waiting while they saved up for a house. It was different for him. They already had a place; they didn't want a long engagement. Now he admits that maybe he should have been like his sister and listened to his parents. The wisdom of hindsight!

The second time around, however, he was much more open to the idea of caution and he actively sought his parents' opinions, especially his mother's because she seemed more interested in giving relationship advice, albeit coloured by what she saw as her husband's failings.

"Your father was much more interesting when we were courting. Once we were married, it was as if he switched off. Now he'd got a wife to cook and clean for him, he could relax and go to sleep. His job was done. When you're dating a girl, you've got to really get to know her and see into the future. What's she going to be like once she's got her claws into you? You didn't know that the first time around, did you? I could see what was coming but you couldn't."

It probably helped that his parents actually liked his new girlfriend — she was his first in a long time since the divorce — and she, in turn, made a big effort to connect with them.

"Tammy's such a nice girl. She talks to us like she's known us all her life. That's a good sign. So many marriages go off the rails because one of them, or maybe both of them, really can't stand their in-laws. You've always got to get your mother-in-law onside."

Anyway, he had learnt his lesson. Over-learnt it because when he met Tamara, who was to become his second wife, he took so long to commit that he almost lost her. He often quizzed her about her past boyfriends. He persisted so much with his probe that she threatened at one stage to end their relationship. For a day or two he also hovered on the brink of breaking it off. He felt she must be hiding something and he didn't want to make another mistake. Or she was overreacting as a sign that she was going to be high mainte-nance. He reasoned that asking about her previous boyfriends was just taking an interest in her life rather than making it all about him. Girls liked guys to take an interest, didn't they? But he relent-ed, gave her the benefit of the doubt and she got over it.

When she asked about his first marriage, however, he never told her what his first wife blamed for the break-up and he certainly never repeated the "sullen killjoy" accusation. He worried that such revelations would put her off. Once she even asked him directly what his first wife's version of the story was. He got quite prickly about that and brushed it off by saying that they just had different priorities and drifted apart. Luckily, she accepted that and has never returned to the subject.

Apart from that one all-important time of going blindly into marriage and not thinking it through, there haven't been any bad consequences of operating on automatic pilot mode over routine things — like locking doors. It was just that one time when he switched off and married without due care and attention. He didn't really understand then how hard he had to think about relationships and work at them; all relationships whether those with friends, col-leagues or a lover. He didn't look carefully enough at the map, where he should have seen the sharp bends and dangerous intersections on the road ahead. All these required full engagement, not automatic pilot. Now he gets it.

It was eye-opening for him to come to the realisation after his divorce that we learn most about relationships from our parents. He got that from a course Tamara insisted on them doing together. It was just before they got married and was specifically about second marriages. He resisted because he didn't like courses — he'd wasted countless hours doing enforced management courses at work — but he reluctantly agreed to do this one just to keep his fiancée happy. To his surprise, it was a revelation.

For one thing, it explained how our parents are our childhood role models. What they do becomes normal life for their children and is a major influence on the way they, in turn, behave. Unfortunately, parents like his weren't the greatest role models. Their "normal" is anything but that. His parents have stayed together but rarely does a day pass without them arguing. They talk to each other as if they are sworn enemies, forever critical of each other and making no attempt to hide it from the children. Just as he did in the end with his ex-wife, fighting with her and constantly criticising her. He'd not seen the connection with his childhood experiences.

His ex's own parents weren't much better. Hers was a dysfunctional family. Her mother had a quite serious drinking problem and the parents split up not long before he met their daughter. So neither he nor his fiancée brought great parental role-modelling of relationship skills into their marriage. To his own parents' credit though, for all their faults, they could see that their first prospective daughter-in-law would be hard work. Maybe it really does take one to know one.

Now his second marriage is going much better. He feels that he's learnt from the failure of his first marriage and is more aware of potential pitfalls. No more automatic pilot. Indeed, he understands himself and others better than his younger self did. Take the question of whether or not to have children. He has a niggling suspicion that his wife will change her mind about having children. They've talked about having kids and they are on the same page — they don't want any. She's younger than him — mid-30s — but they both feel they're too old for nappies and kindy. He knows, however, that she's under pressure from her Lebanese family to have children. If she does give in to them, he won't spoil for a fight over it. After all, children are important to women and he would respect that. He definitely doesn't want to get divorced again. Oh well, they'll cross that bridge if they ever get to it.

Still, even though it's been a painful learning curve, he feels confident that his wounds have healed and he's learnt from his mistakes. He's pleased that even though he got suspicious at one time about the nature of the relationship between Tamara and her boss, he's refused to let it bother him and he hasn't let his suspicions get the better of him. It's like a test and he's passed it. He's also tolerated her spending up big on new clothes for the summer. He got very angry when his first wife spent huge amounts on designer labels. He doesn't get angry with Tamara.

There was a test a few weeks ago when he bumped into his ex-wife at the shops and they chatted very amicably. There was no bitterness. Maybe she realises what she's lost now he's moved on to a better relationship. Certainly, he could never have been that civil to her if he'd met her as recently as a year ago, so maybe he too has calmed down and matured. All the same, if he were single and looking for a girlfriend, he would definitely be attracted to Andrea, his ex, whom he met the other day. Not that he will ever say this to Tamara. And he's pretty sure it would have been more than a sexual attraction — not like in his bachelor days. It seemed so easy then. No thought of lasting commitment, no responsibilities, nothing beyond the sex. No need to think about the future but, therefore, blind to it.

So, as he drains the last of his Coke Zero from the can, he feels pleased with himself. Pleased that his marriage breakdown didn't stop him from wanting to try again with another woman because, by then, he was no longer on automatic pilot or seduced by sex. He's confident this time his marriage will endure, though he remembers only too well assuming that his first marriage was forever. But he's smarter now. That's the big difference.

Then again, maybe not as smart outside of marriage.

His lunchtime musing suddenly goes off track as yesterday's work disaster returns to haunt him. If only he had not lost his temper when frustration with his boss boiled over. He said some things that he really wouldn't, and shouldn't, have said if he'd not been so angry at her for knocking back his project proposal. She's an amateur, promoted out of her league. No business brain. No risk taker. He's been in this game much longer than her and his idea was a sure-fire winner. Admittedly, there were risks, but nothing in business comes without risk. The meeting ended acrimoniously and shortly afterwards he got an email, summoning him to a meeting with her and the big boss next week. Now he can hear the creepy music that movies always use when something bad is about to happen. It's not that she didn't deserve what he said but he should have been smart enough to know that nothing good will come out of giving in to his anger. Not with a woman as thin-skinned as her. Now he worries that he's blown apart his previously OK relationship with her like a failed suicide bomber who kills no one except himself.

Next week when he faces the music at work, he's going to need some of those relationship skills that have helped him so much since his divorce. Maybe think of her as his wife and put aside his anger for the good of the marriage. Ha, he laughs quietly at the thought of being married to his boss. She'd be the last woman on earth that he would ever contemplate marrying. He doubts whether she's ever attracted the interest of any would-be suitor. A spinster ahead of her time!

No, he has to stop thinking like that. He's got to back off. Admit he made a mistake. Think of the bigger picture — the need to keep his job. As he rises from his seat to go back to work across the road, he tells himself he can do this. Talk himself out of trouble. He's faced bigger tests and come through them alright. He can do this. And he really should tell Tammy what's happened, get her onside. She will be a great support. Hopefully. He would never have told Andrea. Too proud. He's so lucky to have Tammy.

Oh, and he did close the back door after all! Both in real life and metaphorically.

FRIENDLY FIRE

*Those who are not agreeable toward you must be
regarded as those who are congenial and pleasant
so that, perchance, this darkness of disagreement
and conflict may disappear from amongst men and
the light of the divine may shine forth, so that the
Orient may be illumined and the Occident filled
with fragrance, nay, so that the East and West
may embrace each other in love and deal with one
another in sympathy and affection. Until man
reaches this high station, the world of humanity
shall not find rest, and eternal felicity shall not
be attained.*

— 'Abdu'l-Bahá, The Promulgation of Universal Peace

JAMILA WAS IN her first year of university, the youngest of two
children and her parents' only daughter. She was her mother's little
girl. If only she were still a little girl as far as her father was concerned. Her skin was a dusky Persian hue and the thin coating of

dark hair on her arms was defiantly unshaven. Her smile lit up any room that she entered. Her father had convinced himself that no boy could ignore her and he worried about the kind of attention she might attract. That's why he wished she were a child again.

One morning at breakfast her smile was missing as three times she refused to eat any of her mother's offerings and made do with just a date and a cup of Persian tea. As she sat at the kitchen bench, she busily worked her smartphone, ran a hand through her long black hair and took occasional sips of her tea. Throughout it all, her phone never left her hand.

"So, what did you do last night, Jamila joon?" her mother asked, not yet willing to admit defeat in her attempt to feed her daughter.

"Nothing much."

"Where did you go?"

"A new bar in Subi."

"Who did you see?"

"Friends."

"What friends?"

"Look, you don't subject my brother to interrogations like this. Why do I get special treatment?"

"Is it a crime for a mother to want to know what her daughter did last night?"

Jamila was getting increasingly irritated.

"All right, all right, I'll file a detailed written report later if you like. Just. Stop. Bugging. Me. Mother!"

If she intended her sarcasm as a way to get her mother off her case, it didn't work. Her Persian *maman* never took notice of such warnings. Again, she insisted that Jamila needed to eat something and thrust a packet of cereal at her daughter.

"Stop it!" Jamila shouted. "Please leave me alone."

Furiously, she finished her tea, slammed the cup down and made to leave the kitchen. Her father, who had immersed himself in the morning paper's sports pages, rose from the table and blocked her path.

"Cut that out, my girl! You don't talk to your mother like that. What's your problem?"

Although thunder seemed about to break as Jamila stared ominously at him, somehow she restrained herself from saying anything. But then the thunder rolled inward. She screwed up her eyes, lowered her head and almost threw herself, sobbing, into her father's startled arms. Her mother rushed in and wrenched her away. Grabbing her tightly around the waist with one arm, she guided the back of her head into her shoulder with the other arm.

"There, there, sweet girl, what's all this about? What's upset you? … Here, I have tissue … Edward, give me water … Take your time, dearest."

Jamila duly did take lots of time to answer her mother's questioning. Her father stealthily stole a few sideways glances at the sports pages — he didn't like cliffhanger silences. Her mother hovered, prepared to wait all day for an explanation if necessary. Eventually, Jamila lifted her head off her mother's tear-sodden shoulder.

"It was Nathan. I liked him. Really liked him. I thought he liked me but last night he called me a Muslim — I won't tell you what else he called me — and said: 'You people just can't be trusted.'"

Her mother pulled her back into her shoulder and stroked Jamila's shiny hair with a firm hand.

"I hope you called him a bloody idiot," said her father, wading bravely into the sea of feminine emotion. "Tell me where he lives and I will go — "

"Please no, Edward, that will only put oil on fire," his wife said, disarming him as she always did with her Persian version of English.

"No one says something like that to my daughter and gets away with it scot-free." His wife had doused the fire and he was talking harmlessly to himself. "That's the trouble these days

— no one stands up to scumbags. Everyone wants to be politically correct. Well, the only thing necessary for the triumph of evil is for good men to do nothing. Don Burke said that and he was bang on the money."

"*Edmund* Burke," Jamila corrected him with a hint of a smile.

Just then Jamila's older brother, Sam, appeared, looking more asleep than awake. He flicked a bleary-eyed glance at his sister entwined in a tearful embrace with her mother.

"What's up, sis? Choking on your cornflakes again?"

Jamila pulled away from her mother with a disgusted look on her face and deliberately bumped into him as she made to leave the kitchen. "You're such a loser."

Ted had a weekly lunchtime pub session with his three mates, Wes, Robbie and "Lurch". They all worked in the city and had been devout in their commitment to meeting every Tuesday at the Federal Hotel. But Ted never shared with Mitra much of what the four friends discussed. Today Ted was telling them about his daughter's brush with bigotry. "She followed him out the door and told him full on what a prick he was," he said with considerable embellishment. "She's going to report him to the police ... she'll name and shame him on Facebook."

"People think they can say anything they like these days."

"She's not even a Muslim!"

"It's bullying plain and simple."

Bullying. Ted remembered bullies from his schooldays.

"Yeah, when I was at school, the class bully used to pick on the weak ones but me and my mates got him back big time. We slipped some hash into his desk and dobbed him in. He was suspended and never came back."

"We resolved things with our fists."

"If anyone insulted your girl the way that guy did, the teachers would have sorted him out."

"No one in my day would have slagged off a beautiful girl like yours."

They were back in the familiar sunshine of Memory Lane, where life is always simpler and better.

On Mitra's day off from her job as a hospital nurse, she phoned her best friend, Fariba, and invited her round. As always, Mitra prepared Persian tea and a lavish selection of cake and fruit, augmented by pistachio nuts and Turkish delights that Fariba brought with her. The two Iranians caught up like this at least once a week. The women, both Bahá'ís, grew up together in Shiraz and came to Australia as refugees with their families after the Iranian revolution saw the start of religious persecution. The friends were just children then and both met their husbands in Australia. Despite her parents' initial reluctance, Mitra married Edward, a fourth-generation Australian, while Fariba married another Iranian refugee.

Mitra and Fariba always turned to each other in times of crisis. Sometimes Mitra's problems revolved around frustration with her husband. He didn't oppose her religious involvement but he doggedly refused to share those same beliefs. She had never anticipated this. He was a good man and, in her mind, it was inevitable that all good people would become Bahá'ís like her. She loved it when Jamila challenged him about religion and easily dismantled his arguments. This stoked Mitra's undying optimism that one day he would join the religion. She considered Jamila a perfect daughter who could do no wrong. Fariba had heard a rumour about Jamila but she kept it to herself.

This time Jamila was at the centre of Mitra's crisis. She told Fariba what had happened with the boy and how his outburst had crushed Jamila. "Her heart has broke in a thousand pieces," she said dramatically. She went even further, adding how worried she was that her daughter might be "damaged for life". Fariba was the consummate consoler, clasping Mitra's hand and agreeing enthusiastically with everything she said. Then, when emotion got the better of Mitra, Fariba coiled both arms round her friend's shoulders and they switched into Farsi.

"Inshallah, man bayad baraye hefazate dokhtare azizam har kari bokonam. (Inshallah, I must do everything to protect my beloved daughter.)"

"Bale, bale. (Yes, yes.)"

"Farzande dokhtar ehtiyaj be eshghe mother dareh. (A girl needs her mother's love.)"

"Albatteh, yek dokhtar hichvaght anghadar pir nashodeh ke natoneh roye shoneh motharesh geryeh koneh ya motharesh ro baghal nakoneh. (Of course, a girl never grows too old to cry on her mother's shoulder or to be hugged by her.)"

"Man brash doa mikonam. Fariba joon shoma ham brash doa mikoni?" ("I will pray for her. Will you pray too, Fariba joon?")

"Albatteh, lazem nist beporci. inshallah jamilia joon harfhaye in pesare bi adab ra faramosh mikoneh. (Of course. You don't have to ask. Inshallah, Jamila joon will forget what this terrible boy said.)"

Jamila always shared her troubles with her best friend, Mona. She was two years older but Jamila had known her for many years through their religion. When she told Mona what had happened, the response surprised her.

"Just ignore it. A bigot doesn't change. Nothing you do will make him change. If you get angry with him, it will make it worse. He will say even worse things to you and to his friends. Don't react."

That wasn't how Jamila viewed it. "But then he will carry on and behave like that towards others. He needs to know that it's wrong."

"Racists are not going to stop being racists. Don't waste your time trying to change him. Move on."

Jamila didn't want to move on and she baulked when her mother told her repeatedly to "forget him" and "he doesn't deserve one second more of your time." She started smothering her daughter with endearments and generally fussed over her as if she were trying to put a baby to sleep. Not that this "baby" could be coaxed to sleep. Jamila had never been one to walk away from a problem. God knows, she'd never let her father get away with unacceptable comments. After hearing a rumour that she had slept with a boy from school, she'd confronted the so-called friend who had been the source of the rumour and snuffed it out. So she grew more and more determined to confront Nathan. In that way, she was like her father, but it was a non-violent confrontation she had in mind.

She texted Nathan, asking him to meet her for coffee that afternoon. "Busy," he replied. She wouldn't take no for an answer and suggested the next day but he couldn't meet her then either. "When will you not be busy?" she asked. "Nothing to talk about," he replied. So Jamila decided she would have to force him into conversation with a face-to-face confrontation, a move that risked another withering put-down. Still, her determination was greater than her fear.

Her chance came a few days later when she saw him sitting on the grass at uni with four friends — one of them a friend of

Jamila's, Sian, who was safely Caucasian like him. She approached from behind and plonked herself down in the narrow space between Nathan and Sian.

"Hi, Nate, you can't avoid me forever."

He looked at her with indifference and said nothing.

Sian, oblivious to the history and assuming that Jamila's comment was just friendly joking, changed the subject.

"Nice jeans, Jammy."

"Not nice enough for Nate, I'm afraid."

Nathan rose to the bait. "What is this? I couldn't care less about your jeans."

"That is unless a girl needs help to get out of her jeans," Lucas, one of three boys in the group, joked and all three sniggered.

"Not funny, Lucas," Jamila said in such a forceful way that it silenced the laughter. "Not funny either that the other day Nate called me 'a Muslim bitch who supports terrorists'."

He shook his head. "I said no such thing."

"Don't try and lie about it. You so did say it."

"I'm not going to listen to this bullshit."

With that, he jumped up, grabbed his bag and stalked off. One of the boys, Dino, stared at Jamila and didn't say anything.

"What?" she snapped.

"Seriously, did he say that about you, that you were a rag-head terrorist?"

"Yes, he did, but at least he had the decency to call me a Muslim, not a raghead. Raghead is a deeply offensive term."

"Yeah, yeah, I'm sorry. You're not a rag-, a Muslim, though, are you?"

"No, I'm a Bahá'í and I don't support killing people in the name of religion. True religion should bring people together."

"I thought so. I'll talk to Nate."

He went off in pursuit of Nathan. Jamila wasn't sure what to make of Dino. She knew him but not well and it'd always seemed like his first allegiance was to the boys.

"If I didn't know better, I'd say Dino was trying to impress you," said Sian. "But he's gay so he's not interested in you in that kind of way."

"He's gay?" Jamila didn't know that.

"Well, that's the rumour and he's never been known to have had a girlfriend."

"I wouldn't necessarily believe gossip. There's probably a rumour going round that I'm a stuck-up Muslim who supports ISIS."

"There is!"

"And I'm not!"

Later that day Jamila received a text from Nathan. It was an apology. He admitted saying the things to her that he'd earlier denied ever saying. He said sorry and that day had been "a bad one for me" and he had taken it out on her. As apologies go, it was minimal. There was no big "how can I make it up to you?"; no details about his bad day; no acknowledgement that he'd probably been talked into it by Dino. Worst of all, he was hiding behind a text instead of apologising to her face. Texts were easier.

Jamila started writing a text back to him, accepting the apology and suggesting they have a coffee. Then she decided to delete it and instead, she rang him. Her call went straight to voicemail: "Hi, Nate. I got your text. Thanks for apologising and let's just forget the other day ever happened. We're friends. Do you want to tell me about your bad day?"

There was an instant text reply.

"Thanks, but no thanks. I don't want to talk about it. Catch you later."

Jamila persisted and Nathan continued to resist. But it was a good-natured texting "conversation" and Jamila felt emboldened to invite him for a coffee.

"Tomorrow at 10 at Gesha," Jamila texted. "My shout. See you there."

There was no response. The next day, a Saturday, Jamila made sure she was at the café by 10 — she wasn't usually known for her punctuality. She sat at a corner table from which she could see everyone who entered the café. The minutes ticked by and there was no sign of Nathan. She was about to give up on him when he finally appeared. She stood and waved. With an old cap skew-whiff on his head and his long fair hair bouncing around on his shoulders, he smiled sheepishly. As she watched him weave his way towards her, through the queue at the counter, she wondered what her mother would make of him if they ever got into a serious relationship. He definitely wouldn't be her mother's idea of a son-in-law. He apologised for being late and Jamila ribbed him by talking up her punctuality, but Nathan countered by rightly observing that she had never before turned up on time for anything, even exams. The banter set them both at ease.

As promised, Jamila insisted on coffee being her shout and when she returned to their table after ordering at the counter, they chatted generally for a few minutes about their studies and what they had planned for the long summer holidays. Fairly quickly, a waitress brought their coffees and then Jamila dived below the conversation's polite surface.

"So, what was it all about?" she asked. "Your bad day?"

He visibly squirmed. "You don't need to know."

"It must have been something heavy for you to react the way you did."

"I say stupid things sometimes."

"You certainly do but that wasn't you at all. What upset you that day?"

Again, he avoided answering the question. "Why are you so keen to know?"

"It's what friends do. They talk and help each other out."

"Not my friends. We keep things light. Have a laugh."

"I'm a friend and I'm not laughing. What was it?"

"I don't want to talk about it."

"Don't you trust me?"

"It's not that."

"Then what is it?"

"You're asking me to spill my guts and no one's ever asked me to do that."

"Sounds like you really don't have any friends!"

"Geez Louise, thanks for that! Look, I was incredibly rude to you the other day. So why are you doing this?"

"Because we're friends, Nate. We had a falling out. We're good now. And I want to know why my friend was so upset."

There was silence. Nathan took a couple of sips of his long black.

"Wow, they do good coffee here," he said, gazing in admiration at his cup.

"Stop avoiding the issue, Nate. You — "

"My parents have broken up. I didn't see it coming."

LETTERS OF FAITH

*Handwritten letters often feel more intimate
than a conversation. It's the soul flung wide;
unlike real life where so often we fold the
wings over us. Hiding behind our boasts and
glibness and slippery untruths.*
— Nikki Gemmell, The Weekend Australian

KIERAN HAD FOUND the letters bundled together stiffly with an elastic band at the back of a drawer in the bedroom when he began the process of cleaning out his parents' house. His mother's letters looked as if they hadn't been touched since the year of the most recent postmarks, 1969. There were maybe 15 of them, all addressed by hand to "Miss Nicolette Moyes". Kieran carefully removed the elastic band. He did so tentatively, not wanting to tear anything ... or anyone. The letters seemed to be locked together, having lain undisturbed for many years; prising them apart made him feel guilty — as if he were exhuming a body, and in a way he was. His mother was dead and now his father, too. It felt wrong to pry into their drawers and lives. All the same, he couldn't resist.

The letters had been arranged methodically in order of their postmarks, first to last. After a few moments of hesitation, he opened the first of them, posted in Perth on Friday, April 5, 1968, to "Sweetest Nicky" from "The Man Who Worships You, Joe". Kieran started reading. It was a love letter from his father to his mother.

"From the very first moment I saw you in that room, wearing that red dress and impish smile and asking all the questions, I knew. I wanted to be with you so much. I wanted to touch you, to hold you … "

Kieran turned away and stared at the blank wall. This was prying and painful. A defenceless father's private sexual desire made public. It was his father being emotionally open, something he had rarely, if ever, seen from him. This didn't sound like his father.

" … but this is not physical attraction alone (although there's a lot of that!). No, it is so much more. This is love. What makes it so is the spiritual fire you have lit in my life. You light up a world I didn't know existed. I am overwhelmed by your devotion, your selflessness, your total belief, your determination to ignite the whole material world with this spark and to bring everything together in unity before God — all of these things make me love you with a new kind of passion."

Kieran felt like a detective looking for evidence at a crime scene. Evidence of what? A crime of passion? The letters had been written almost 50 years ago. What exactly was he hoping to find among these words of love from his father, who died last month, to his mother, who died last year? For a long time he had seen his parents as two old people tut-tutting about young people's irresponsibility and unhealthy obsession with mobile phones. Now it came as a jolt, an electric shock, to see them as free-spirited youths and his father, effectively, making love in writing.

Kieran quickly found, however, that the letter, though centred on his father's feelings for his mother, offered other insights.

For one thing, it gave him a sense of the way his parents' times affected them. He wrote it just after learning of the assassination of American civil rights leader Martin Luther King. While Kieran knew that the shock of this event reverberated around the world, he was surprised at the impact it had on his father.

"I've just heard the terrible news that Dr King is dead, shot dead in Memphis," Joe wrote. *"You know how much I admired him, Nicky. He was my hero and yours, too. And now he's gone. Still, after walking around for a few hours in a daze, I've begun to think of his loss as the very reason why it's all the more important that we keep his dream alive. We must take up his revolution of peace and brotherhood and equality. We need that spiritual revolution to transform not just America but the whole world. I think you understand this more than anyone I know."*

Kieran knew that she would "understand" because of his parents' spiritual beliefs and values. Kieran's mother was a Bahá'í and introduced his father to her faith when she met him in Melbourne. Kieran knew that it was some sort of chance meeting in a pub but his parents never told him the full story of that fateful encounter and he'd never had sufficient curiosity to ask. Now, reading these letters, he finally found the curiosity — too late. What pub? How did they both come to be there? Did they start dating straight away? He didn't know the answers and he feared that he wasn't going to find them in these letters.

This first letter — written the day before his father left his hometown of Perth — also talked a lot about his forthcoming trip overseas. He was planning to spend the northern summer travelling around Europe. He didn't know how long he would be gone. It depended on how long his money would last and "how long I can survive without seeing you". He was feeling daunted about the trip and wishing they could have travelled together but "I know it would be stupid for you to give up your first teaching job."

Next in the chronological batch was a postcard of Big Ben, posted on Monday, April 8, 1968. It was posted the day after he got to London and his first letter from overseas followed two weeks later. It spoke of how much Joe was missing "my darling Nicky". He was in London seeing the world and "hanging out with hippies" who talked about a revolution of peace and love. "Man, London's a really groovy scene. If only you could be here to share it with me. I wish that more than anything. Everyone wants to change the world, and the music — oh, man!"

Kieran stared at the bone-dry paper. His hand held his father's heart. Yet he felt he had known only the reserved man, the parent who rarely surrendered to emotion, who hid his heart from his son and never spoke about his time in London. Instead, he used to give Kieran little coded "I love you" messages. Messages like a model aeroplane, the perfect birthday present, that he'd spent hours hunting down for him in unfamiliar places or, in the days before Kieran had a car and was still at school, the drives without complaint to take him to a party and then all the way back to collect him late at night. Joe often hugged his son when greeting or farewelling him but he never seemed relaxed in such moments of intimacy, not like he was in these letters.

Kieran read slowly, taking long pauses between sentences, searching for his father and sifting his words for clues, then returning to various points in the letter and reflecting on what he'd read with long silent stares. Weary to the point of exhaustion after just two letters, Kieran carefully folded them back into their envelopes, returned them with the postcard to the top of the bundle and put the elastic band back around them. He placed the letters and the rubber band exactly in their original positions on top of each other, slotted perfectly into the tiny cracks and curls of the bundle. It looked as if nothing had been disturbed. But it had.

He took the letters home with him and placed them reverently next to a picture of his parents in his bedroom as if placing an offering at the foot of a religious icon. That night he couldn't sleep because it felt as if a stranger were in the room watching him. The stranger was his father. In his sleepless discomfort, Kieran was plagued by the whole question of religious identity — his parents' and his lack of it.

He grew up immersed in the Bahá'í Faith, which his parents followed. He was comfortable with it as a child because it seemed the normal thing to do. Then in his teens he realised, religion wasn't the normal thing to do. None of his school friends had any religious convictions, at least none they were prepared to reveal, and he retreated from the challenge of talking about his religion or defending it. It would turn him into an outsider. With those who knew his family, he kept his distance from the Faith by making it his parents' religion rather than his own. His lifelong immersion, which in theory should have strengthened him in it, left him floundering. He didn't believe sufficiently in the no-sex-before-marriage of his parents' faith to be the only one among his friends not sleeping with girls. Away from his parents, he abandoned other core beliefs. He still believed in God but wanted to believe in his own way. He stopped going to most Bahá'í meetings. He could see the disappointment in his mother's eyes at his pulling away. Although she did not give up trying to coax him into going to meetings, she never pushed him too hard as if frightened of breaking his fragile veneer of faith.

Soon after Kieran first started moving away from the religion, his father got into one of his occasional belligerent moods and tried to goad him back into the fold. "You need spiritual backbone in this world," he bellowed but sounded to Kieran like a dinosaur putting on one last show of strength. Kieran didn't respond.

Kieran often wondered why his parents did not raise the subject with him again after that. They must have been upset at the direction he was taking … or perhaps, Kieran reasoned, they completely missed the obvious. After all, they missed the drug habit he developed in his mid-twenties and drugs were forbidden in the Bahá'í Faith. It was like so many things in his relationship with his parents: they didn't talk about it. As girlfriends came and went, his parents didn't pry or ask too much about the break-ups. They always accepted the girlfriends he brought round to meet them, even troubled Belle, who later took an overdose and nearly died. Not that Kieran told them that, of course. His parents didn't ask and Kieran didn't tell. These uncrossed bridges in his family had always troubled him and now that his parents lived only in these old letters, Kieran was beginning to regret all those years of ungrasped opportunities.

Over the next week, he spent many hours with the stranger lurking in the letters. He took the letters to his living room and read them there with lengthy gaps between each letter. A very long pause for thought. He read each one repeatedly, dissecting every sentence for deeper insights. They chronicled his father's summer of travelling around Europe. They spoke of eccentric characters he met, beautiful places he visited, flea-ridden beds in which he slept and his yearning for the woman he loved on the other side of the world.

"We went to a club, drank a lot and listened to some fabulous jazz," he wrote from Paris in August 1968. *"An American girl from the hostel cemented herself at my side. We talked about things that matter ('Can analysis be worthwhile? Is the theatre really dead?') and she was funny. In the days before I met you, I would probably have hooked up with her but I wasn't even slightly tempted because I'm interested only in you. You're constantly in my thoughts. God, I wish you were here with me but even though you're not, I would never cheat on you."*

Then the letter turned to spiritual matters.

"*This morning I read some of the Hidden Words book that you gave me (thanks again for this wonderful gift — it's been my daily inspiration, helping me to 'unravel the mysteries of love from its windflowers') and I read this: 'Strive that your deeds may be cleansed from the dust of self and hypocrisy and find favour at the court of glory; for ere long the assayers of mankind shall, in the holy presence of the Adored One, accept naught but absolute virtue and deeds of stainless purity.'*

"*Wow, 'accept naught but absolute virtue and deeds of stainless purity'!!!! That must be my aim now. I've got a lot to make up for. I used to aim so low and missed even that miserable mark.*"

As Kieran mulled over these words, he saw that his father, rather than cleansing himself from "the dust of self", was actually full of self. The letter was all about him. But then wasn't Kieran himself just as covered in this same dust as his father had been? Going through these letters was more about Kieran's own preoccupations than about his father's worries all those years ago.

When he read a very different letter sent from Madrid, however, Kieran found that his father's enthusiasm for "stainless purity" had waned. "*How can I possibly live up to that standard?*" Joe mused, again introspectively. "*I'm worried that this is just another version of religion sitting in judgment on people.*"

This felt creepy. And he knew it was not just from prying into his father's private thoughts when his father was no longer around to explain himself. His father was now concerned that religion was setting impossibly high standards and this, too, was one of the issues that had prised Kieran away from his parents' faith. Not having sex outside marriage, for example, was all well and good in theory but, as a teenager, he had felt it was impossible to achieve and an unnecessary burden to impose on a young person.

"*I'm always falling far short,*" the letter went on, "*and how could I claim to follow a set of religious teachings if I failed to live* them? I'd have the constant guilt of advocating for others, standards that I didn't practise myself."

But again, he looked to Kieran's mother for an answer: "Still, my beautiful mentor, perhaps you can get me through this self-doubt."

Kieran stopped and made himself a strong black coffee. As he drank, he recalled the time he parted company with religion and opened up about it to no one but his sister, his only sibling, two years older than him. Kieran swallowed hard as his thoughts travelled back to Kathy's smile. They were close. They shared secrets and actively sought each other's opinion of boyfriends or girlfriends. Although she didn't share any of his anxiety about their family's faith, she didn't judge or condemn him for his discomfort … But at the age of 20, just a few months after he confided in her, Kathy was gone, killed in a car accident. Her death crushed his family. As Kieran toyed listlessly with his cup, he made a conscious effort not to think any more about Kathy.

When he veered away from religion, he didn't flounce away histrionically; he didn't even resign from the religion. He just kept finding excuses for not going to meetings. He started drinking — not heavily — but it seemed clear to Kieran that his parents had no idea what he was getting up to at night. They were too weighed down with grief over his sister's death to notice. Kieran couldn't bring himself to tell them he didn't believe in their religion anymore. He figured that it would cause a huge upset and he imagined his lawyer father getting angry, running rings around him with eloquent legalistic argument and making him feel humiliatingly small.

Avoidance became his habit as he carried on living his double life. He succeeded in hiding from his parents the smell of alcohol and evidence of his outlawed activities. But these deceits were mere tokens of deeper currents. Intimidated by his parents' conviction and devotion, and wounded by his sister's death, he hid his true feelings from them.

Now, however, this letter was showing him a father he'd never met. One who had questioned the religion and come through later with his faith intact and strong. If only Kieran had asked more questions and his father had opened up to him about his own experiences, it could have made such a difference. Instead, here he was, 39, token religious, constantly torn by feelings of hypocrisy and adrift. Guilt and its accomplice, fear, followed him everywhere; guilt that he was failing God and fear that he would be judged accordingly. He wasn't being true to himself or true to God.

Kieran came to a six-week gap in the letters. Then in October 1968, his father was back in London and running out of money. *"Maybe I'll be back in Australia soon. Can't wait to see you,"* he said.

Sure enough, the next letter was written from Australia — but from Perth, his hometown, and not Melbourne, where Kieran's mother lived. Kieran's parents had just seen each other in Melbourne and his father was apologising profusely about "Angelina".

His father must have had an affair! He was as good as married by then and yet here he was coming clean and admitting to having been with another woman! Again, his father had proved unpredictable. Just as he had gone from enthusiastic acceptance of the Bahá'í Faith's ideals to doubting them, now here he was cheating on the woman he loved after telling her that he would never be tempted by other women. The letter was short on detail but Kieran's mother obviously must have forgiven him and they lived happily ever after because they married three months later. He had proposed to her in Melbourne — *"I can't wait until we are united in marriage."*

But, intriguingly, the letter also referred to something happening around that time that caused his mother to question her Bahá'í beliefs. His father was sure she would get through "this time of doubt" because she had "such a deep faith" and that she would grow stronger because of "the attack" on her. Again, though, there was insufficient detail and no letters from his mother to explain fully what had happened. It was also the last of the letters. Kieran would have loved to have known how they dealt with both the affair and the attack on his mother ... more missed opportunities.

His mother's problem must have been serious because his father also wrote: *"At first, I didn't know how to respond about your issue. Please forgive me, I'm asking for a lot of forgiveness, I know, but I thought if even you were beset by doubt, what hope was there for me?"*

Kieran smiled at this. Right to the last, his father was self-centred. This wasn't the father he remembered who, when it came to work, always put others' needs ahead of his own and who worked deep into the early hours of the morning on other people's problems. But the letter also said something that Kieran took as an encouraging sign:

"Having thought about it a lot more since then, I now see that this is not just a question of how your spiritual state affects me. I'm hoping that you can see it all as an opportunity for us both to make our spiritual journey together, sharing the challenges and doubts. We can help each other, support each other and 'immerse yourselves in the ocean of My words, that ye may unravel its secrets and discover all the pearls of wisdom that lie hid in its depths'".

So the letters had thrown up mysteries and unanswered questions. They had portrayed his parents, particularly his father, as people he didn't recognise. At 39, Kieran's youthful rebellion had cooled and left him with that empty feeling you get when a fire burns itself out. It was compounded by the loss of both his parents in relatively quick succession. Having also lost his sister, he had no immediate family left and he had no wife to fill the gap. He was fighting the emptiness on his own. He had long wished he could be as strong in his convictions as he had known his parents to be and yet these letters revealed that he didn't know his parents very well at all.

The only relative he really had left was his aunt and he decided to talk to her about the letters. More especially, he wanted to talk to her about what wasn't in the letters. He had never talked to her about family matters of such a sensitive nature and he wasn't sure she'd have, or be willing to give, the answers to his questions. In particular, he wanted to quiz her on his mother's period of doubt about her faith. He was curious how she managed to carry on regardless with her faith. Something he had been unable to do.

His mother's older sister was the last surviving sibling of his parents on either side: his father's brother and sister were both dead and neither of them married; Meg and his mother had no other siblings. Aunt Meg's apartment by the river wasn't far away and he often saw her. He had always got on well with Meg, but not to the extent of talking much about deep subjects. She was now in her early 70s and wasn't religious. Kieran saw her as a silent co-conspirator who understood religion's excessive demands and rejected them, but without bitterness and without criticism of his parents' choices. That led him to think that she probably wouldn't tell him anything now that would, in any way, be critical of her sister and brother-in-law. Meg knew that he drank but he had never told her about his drug-taking. He suspected, however, that Meg had a few secrets of her own, too.

He smiled to himself as he thought of Meg's slim, young look even though she had given up a couple of years ago on dyeing her hair and was now grey. She was more active than women half her age. She swam, played bowls and, until her knees started giving her trouble a couple of years ago, she used to be a serial walker who thought nothing of walking three kilometres to the shops. There was still a youthfulness about her thinking. Watching the footy on television, she screeched like a teenager with excitement or despair. Unlike many of her age, she did not talk endlessly about the Sixties and drool over the music from that long-lost era. She listened to Triple J and liked a lot of contemporary music. Meg had never married but, like Kieran, she had had one or two serious relationships over the years. No one, Kieran guessed, was good enough for her.

Meg and Kieran's mother had been close but not in matters of religion or politics. Whereas his mother was apolitical and religion was the driving force of her life, Meg was vehemently left-wing in her politics. She had never shown any interest in religion, as far as Kieran knew, although she did concede that her sister had chosen one of the more progressive religions.

As he often did, Kieran dropped by uninvited one Saturday morning. She wasn't the sort of relative who demanded you book an appointment to see her. Actually, they had seen a lot of each other this winter following the death of his father. The two deaths in quick succession hit them both hard. Meg admitted she wasn't "good with death" and nor was Kieran but he pretended he could handle it. He had assumed that his parents would be around for much longer. Now they were both dead. He was angry because he hadn't expected that. It wasn't that he had a bad relationship with them, just a distant one, and he had vaguely thought that one day he would get closer to them. Now, as he finally set about trying to do that, he found himself with only his aunt and a bunch of letters.

He smiled as he entered his aunt's unit and saw the familiar mess. Her home overflowed with paperwork, CDs, DVDs, books, ironing and accumulated knick-knacks from her many travels. She made little effort to tidy it all up or to keep the place clean. She was the total opposite of Kieran in this regard; while Kieran ran a brutal housekeeping regime she was a typical Libra.

Pushing aside some battered files bulging with paperwork, Kieran sat on the sofa. He made polite inquiry about his aunt's health, discussed the weather, his aunt's mixed fortunes on the bowling green and the death of a former politician, which had been in the news the night before — they were both avid followers of the news. As if anxious to make up for lost time, Kieran abruptly came to the point of his visit. He told his aunt about the letters. Trying hard not to appear driven, he recounted some of the things his father described in the letters and Meg laughed at the follies of his youth — particularly his dalliance with Angelina.

"Oh, Angelina!" Meg smiled. "I remember hearing about her. I never met her, of course. Sometimes I wondered if Joseph made her up just to get Nic jealous! But he didn't."

"Was Mum jealous?"

"Oh yes. But, actually, Angelina was the best thing that ever happened to Nic. She mopped up all Joseph's hankering after other women. She was too demanding, too intense, too far away."

Kieran asked where she was from?

"Oh, she was from some small town in Spain. On the coast, I think. I'm not sure. From what I gathered afterwards, she was well and truly off Joseph's map. She wasn't the settling-down type. Joseph wouldn't have lasted five minutes with her." Then, as if it was an afterthought, she added: "I wonder what happened to her?"

Since his parents' deaths, Meg was more open to sharing memories about them but Kieran anticipated that he would have to work harder to draw Meg on the deeper question of his mother's spiritual uncertainty all those years ago. And probably it would be to no avail. Meg always went quiet when the conversation turned to religion.

Steering Meg away from Angelina and waiting as long as seemed polite, Kieran finally plunged in and asked what he had gone there to ask.

"My father spoke in his last letter in November '68, just before their marriage, about a mysterious 'attack' that had caused my mother to question some aspect or another of her beliefs. Do you know anything about that? Dad never explained it in his letter and I'm intrigued at the idea of her having any doubt whatsoever about her faith."

Meg hesitated. "Doubt?"

"Yes. In his letter Dad talked about her having a time of doubt and said that she would get through it because she had such a deep faith. I want to know what was going on."

"It sounds like you mean business."

Her tone was quite sharp and Kieran sensed that he had been too pushy. He lowered his voice, hoping to soften his inquisition.

"Well, the letters have shown me a side of my parents I never knew about. I ... " He dithered between opening himself right up and giving nothing away. He was feeling quite agitated but didn't want to sound emotional. Meg smiled.

"Those letters have knocked you about a bit, haven't they?" she said without seeking an answer. She had read him well.

Kieran felt a knot in his throat and could barely say a simple "yes". His show of emotion was clearly visible and seemed to unlock something in Meg.

"It was probably because of me," she said suddenly and paused as if to take in what she had just said. "She'd been talking day after day about this new religion of hers. There was no let-up at all. I wasn't interested but she was on a mission to convert me. I'd tried a couple of times to shake her off. I thought that reminding her repeatedly I didn't believe in God might have been enough but she simply took it as a challenge and redoubled her efforts."

"Yes, that sounds like her," Kieran said ruefully.

"I must admit I was a bit worried about my little sister going all religious on me. There were a lot of dangerous cults preying on people naïve enough to believe in them."

"Did you think Mum was naïve?"

"No." She paused to reconsider. "Maybe. She'd always been *horribly* religious but *reasonably* sensible. Well, she was my sister and look how sensible I am!" Her smile confirmed that she meant the comments jokingly. But now the smile disappeared. "She'd never tried to convert me to any of the many churches she went to at one time or another and I didn't really think she'd fall for one so heavily as she did when she found the Bahá'í Faith. But, goodness me, she started suddenly coming on so strong about this religion that she had me worried. I was worried enough to want to prove it all wrong and protect her. That's what a big sister is supposed to do."

Meg's gaze was fixed on Kieran as she explained that despite the religion advocating equality between the sexes, it restricted membership of its international governing council to men.

"Well, that was the clincher for me. I asked her how she could buy into such hypocrisy and what was the justification for it? It was the only time I ever saw her lost for words and I heard no more about the religion for months after that."

Kieran was surprised that his father had thought of this in his letter as an "attack" and he asked Aunt Meg whether she was sure that her words had cut so deep.

"Oh yes. You know, I even felt bad because she looked so devastated. She wasn't normally one to let me get away with winning a fight!"

Meg's story shook Kieran because this issue about women was also one of the issues that drove him away from the religion. And kept him away. Now he was digesting the discovery that his mother had gone down the very same path but never talked about it. Never shared how she came to terms with this anomaly.

Snapping out of his reverie, Kieran looked up at Meg. "She must have found some sort of answer though because she spent the rest of her life dedicated to the cause and I never ever heard her or Dad doubting any of it."

"You know, in Nic's defence, sometimes there are no rational answers," Meg said. "We can't always find an adequate explanation for everything."

"But, Meg, this is a big issue. It makes a nonsense of everything else the Faith says about women being equal to men."

Meg reached for her mug of tea and took a few, slow sips. Kieran watched her drinking and surmised that she was finding it hard talking like this about her sister. Their family was not in the habit of talking so openly about each other.

For Kieran, this question of women not being allowed on the governing body was too big an issue to ignore but he'd never felt comfortable raising his concerns with his parents or other Bahá'ís. Maybe outsiders could have said the things he wanted to say — as Meg had done — but he felt the argument amounted to betrayal coming from an insider such as him, albeit an insider on the fringes. Here, at last, with Aunt Meg, he felt he had a kindred spirit, someone who might understand his anguish.

Eventually, looking hard into her tea, Meg continued slowly.

"You know, I've always loved my sister dearly and although I had no interest in her religion, I could sort of understand the way she eventually resolved it. Years later we talked about it. She decided that all the other positive things in her faith about the equality of women, which she could understand and accept willingly, were far more significant than the one thing she didn't understand."

To illustrate the point, she talked about her own occasional dilemma about politics.

"You think about it, Kieran. For me, politics is my religion and I don't know of any political party whose full set of policies I totally accept — do you? There's always some policy or decision I don't like. But I have to nail my colours to somebody's mast. Support one party enough to vote for them at an election."

Kieran and his rational mind still weren't satisfied. "But what's so hard about allowing women to belong as members of the top body? They're on the national, regional and local ones — why withhold that one?"

Meg lifted her eyes from her tea and looked over Kieran's shoulder. "Search me, love. Don't forget I don't believe in all this stuff anyway! Your mother told me it was a mystery of God, one that would be better understood sometime in the future but for now, she would just have to have faith in the teaching."

"It was a blind faith," Kieran said, slightly irritated.

"Yes, but we all take leaps of blind faith, don't we?"

She said we all had to have blind faith that the sun would rise every morning and there would be air for us all to breathe. When we drove a car, we had to have blind faith that when we went through a green light, some drunk wouldn't go through the red light and kill us.

Shocked silence. Meg and Kieran stared into each other's startled eyes. This was exactly what had happened to his sister, Kathy, all those years ago. The driver was charged and sentenced to three years in prison. It made the news at the time but ever since then the family had avoided talking about the tragedy. The subject was taboo. Kieran once got angry seeing a story on the news about another drink-driving fatality and when he made the comment to his mother that it was just like what happened to Kathy, she shut him down. She told him she didn't want to be reminded about Kathy's accident and she turned off the TV. He thought it strange at the time but just shrugged and his mother left the room. Now, without thinking, Meg had brought a family tragedy back to life. Neither moved. It was as if they were paralysed.

Hesitantly, Kieran broke the silence and deflected the conversation away from Kathy. "Blind faith can also result in some very bad choices. I had faith in a girl once and it was hopelessly misplaced. She used me, lied to me."

Meg nodded tentatively. "But you can never be certain of anything in life, Kieran, and at some point, you have to leap and hope. Sometimes we make mistakes and hopefully we learn from them. The trick is to know enough about what you're doing so it's not really blind faith. Just calculated faith."

Kieran shifted uneasily in his seat before responding. "When it comes to God though, how can it be anything but blind faith? No one can know for certain that He exists."

Meg rolled her eyes. "You're asking *me* about God? I'm not the one to talk to about that. To me, God is a myth. But if you must throw yourself into believing in God, so be it." It was like deciding a girlfriend or boyfriend was "The One". "You think it through first and go in as aware as possible of what you're committing yourself to. Even then though, there's no guarantee of anything. You basically have to go with your instinct."

"What if you choose caution and don't make a leap of faith?"

"Then you probably miss out on a lot of wonderful discoveries," Meg laughed.

A memory came to Kieran of his mother once saying that Meg was missing out on so much by not believing in God. Kieran thought perhaps Aunt Meg might now be starting to agree — both about God and about men. So, with unusual rashness, Kieran barged into uncharted territory. "What about you? Have you ever been too cautious and missed out?"

"Who hasn't? That's life," Meg said sharply. Her tone made it clear that she wasn't open to discussing the subject and Kieran backed off.

This refusal to discuss sensitive subjects was a family trait. His Dad talked in the letters about his own doubts but never talked about any of that with Kieran.

"You know, I just wish my parents had shared more with me," he said. "It would have been so good to know, when I was a teenager, that their faith didn't come easily to them and that I wasn't such a failure for doubting it all."

Meg took a deep breath and when she spoke, the sharpness was gone from her voice. "I don't reckon it would have made a difference knowing any of this at the age of 18 or 19," she said with a warm smile. "We generally don't want our parents butting in. We think they're out of touch, living in the past and all that. I know I did."

"So finding this out in a letter after they've died is better?" Kieran asked.

The question hung between them …

A few days later, Meg sent Kieran a text that she had something for him and asking if he would be home that night. Kieran had just started dating a work colleague, Rani, from Human Relations, but she was away (not that Meg knew anything about her) and he wasn't doing anything that night. It was about 8 o'clock when his aunt came over.

Meg didn't like the cold and it was a cold winter's night. By the amount of clothes she was wearing, she was rugged up for a temperature of something like -20 but no amount of clothes could thaw the anxiety in her face. Without going through any preliminary niceties, she walked straight in, chose to go no farther than the hallway and, still wearing her heavy winter coat and scarf, pulled a letter out of her handbag.

"Here, I've — I've been thinking about our conversation the other day." She sounded nervous. "I feel bad about a lot of things but I feel particularly bad that I have another letter you've never seen. I would like — I want you to have it." She thrust it abruptly into Kieran's hand hanging loose at his side and he was so taken by surprise that he almost dropped the letter. "Keep it. I won't stop — " She attempted awkwardly to make a smooth turn for the door. "I won't stand over you or anything like that while you read it. I'll be off. It might help you. I hope it does."

Then, before Kieran had a chance to respond, maybe to insist she stay, she was gone. This wasn't like Aunt Meg at all, Kieran thought as he stood alone in the hall. He stared bemused at the writing on the envelope. She had acted so strangely.

He walked slowly into his living room, put Big Brother on mute and sat on the black leather sofa. What could possibly be in this letter to agitate Aunt Meg so much? Would it have the same effect on him? It was 21 years old according to the postmark. Then he saw that it was posted in Perth to Meg's Kalgoorlie address. At that time, Meg, a teacher, was working there. Kieran recognised his mother's writing on the envelope. Then he eagerly pulled out a 14-page typed letter.

"*Dearest, dearest Meg, I don't know where to start. I am so bereft. I've been alone and crying all day. I can't stop. Joe's away, I don't know where Kieran is and even you are nowhere close by. If you were here, I'd sink into your arms and eventually I'd cry myself to a standstill. You'd soothe me (you've always been good at that!) but although it would help so much to have you here, even then you couldn't take away the pain. No one can take that away.*"

Kieran realised what this was about. The letter was written a month after the death of his sister, Kathy.

"*I can't stop thinking about Kathy,*" his mother wrote. "*She was so beautiful. I can't begin to put into words how much I miss her. I keep replaying that terrible night over and over in my head.*"

Even though Meg would have known what happened, Kieran's mother relived it in the letter. She went into such detail that it was as if she was deliberately tormenting herself with endless replays.

The letter told how Kathy went to join her uni friends for coffee in Fremantle but they never showed up —they forgot to tell her that they had decided to go to Claremont instead. After a futile 10-minute wait for them to turn up, Kathy called one of them and found out about the change of plan.

"For some unknown reason, my beautiful daughter, who never went to bed before midnight, decided to have an early night and not bother going to Claremont. It was only 8.30, for God's sake. Then, less than five minutes from home, that moron, that bastard (is there really any word adequate enough to convey what I feel about him?), roared through a red light oblivious to everything and killed her instantly. My beautiful girl, taken horribly from us when she could so easily have been safe in Claremont with her friends."

The letter was one long paragraph of pent-up pain flooding onto the pages. Although Kieran knew that Kathy's death devastated his parents, as was to be expected, he only once saw his mother break down and even then, it was nothing like this silent outpouring of grief. And his mother never saw him cry about it either. He usually did that in private, late at night in bed or parked in some out-of-the-way spot in his car. Only twice did his grief escape in public. This letter took him back to one of those times.

A few days after Kathy died he was in a Myer department store hoping to buy some distraction. He was trying on some pants, looking at himself in the fitting room mirrors, when he started crying. He stood there staring into the face of his grief, unable to hide from it. He had been sobbing audibly for about five minutes when a sales assistant knocked on his door, asking gently what was wrong. Kieran opened the door and, trying to wipe away the tears, blurted out: "It's my sister. She was killed last week in a road accident." Then he lost control all over again and tears streamed anew down his face. He cried into the assistant's shoulder but afterwards, Kieran closed down again, feeling awkward and deeply embarrassed about making a scene in a place like that.

Now, as he paused in reading his mother's letter, with tears again in his eyes, he felt less embarrassed about that day.

Ineffectively wiping away the tears and reading on, Kieran came to a question about halfway through the letter, a question that he could never have imagined his mother asking: "How could God do this to us?" She had picked through the wreckage, looking for God in all this, and He wasn't there. It was a huge shock for Kieran. His mother, whom he had only ever seen as utterly dedicated to her religion, felt betrayed by God.

"Even though I know that death is not the end and that I'll be reunited with Kathy in the next world, right now all I can feel is such an intense grief that I can't find any consolation from thoughts of reunion in the next world. I'll NEVER see her married with her own family, NEVER see her as a fully grown woman. How can anyone deal with something like this? I can't. Most days I just want to die, living is too painful. I've trusted in God all my life, put my whole faith in Him and now He's allowed this to happen. What's the point of serving God if this is what He gives you back by way of thanks?"

Towards the end, the letter talked about him: *"On top of everything, Joe and I still have to put all this behind us and not forget Kieran."*

He braced himself to read something that he wouldn't like — perhaps his mother criticising him or revealing that she knew more about what he'd been doing than he thought she knew.

"He's going through hell as well," she wrote. *"He never shows it but I know. A mother always knows. I think to myself if I'm feeling like I've lost my faith, what's he feeling? My faith has been burning strong for 25 years or so through everything. His little flame of faith is so fragile, so easily blown out. If this had happened to me at his age — I mean, if you'd been killed like Kathy — would I have still held onto my faith?*

I don't know. But now I've got to pull myself together and guide him through all this."

Kieran had never thought of his mother feeling the need to guide him through the loss of his sister and, consumed by his own grief, he had missed his mother's loss of spiritual direction. All he could see at the time was his own bewilderment.

"I don't think I can do it," she continued in the letter. *"I don't think I can honestly tell him soothing words about how God loves us all and we should never stop loving Him. How could you love a God who allows something like this to happen? I don't know if I have it in me to be what Kieran needs me to be, and if I can't do it, who can? Not Joe. Poor man, he's fallen apart too. He's in no state to give out to anyone right now. If anything, I feel like he needs me even more than Kieran does. Damn it, why is it always women who must hold everything together in a calamity? No, there's just no one. It's all down to me!"*

By the end of the 14 pages, Kieran had never wanted so much to talk to his mother but he had missed his chance. All he had was Aunt Meg. Eventually, barely composed, he picked up the phone and rang her. He walked backwards and forwards with agitation as he waited for her to answer. Her phone rang for a long time. When she eventually picked up, her voice was little more than a whisper.

"Aunt Meg, I've just read it." His throat locked and although he tried to say more, no words would come out.

At first, Meg waited for Kieran to continue but then she said something. She sounded as if she was in a trance, thinking aloud and talking to herself.

"This is the thing. She was asking for my help and I couldn't bring myself to give it. Oh yes, I wanted to. So much. Believe me. But it was beyond me. I didn't know where to start. I'm really, really sorry. I should have been there for you, and for Nic and Joe, such lovely people, but I wasn't. I'm so sorry."

Kieran had not seen this coming and this latest shock gave him back his voice.

"No, Aunt Meg, don't blame yourself. We were all struggling pathetically. It's easy to look back now and say, 'I should have done this' or 'I should have done that', but we were paralysed by grief. All of us. Maybe that state of paralysis never left us."

"Nic got through it, Kieran. She dug deeper than any of us and clawed her way out."

"Yes, but how did she ever get through it and not lose her faith?"

There was a long silence. "She did it through prayer and meditation," Meg answered, her whispery voice now growing stronger. "She said that when she did those things, she found new strength. It renewed her faith. I found out a long time afterwards that she sometimes prayed and meditated for an hour or more at a time. Did you know that? You probably didn't. She probably did this when you weren't around. She often went to Kings Park for that reason but you wouldn't have known anything about that. She wanted to keep her grief from you. She didn't go back to work for quite a few months after Kathy died and must have been home alone a lot. I wish I could have got that sort of strength from praying and then just sitting there in silence. I've thought a lot about how she managed to, in effect, forgive God. And I think it was because her faith was stronger than her grief."

Kieran sat heavily on the sofa and, closing his eyes, bowed his head. The hand that was holding the phone fell limply onto the seat beside him. Suddenly, he saw the enormity of what his mother had faced alone and overcome alone. He had no idea that Kathy's death almost destroyed his mother's faith and now he saw that she deliberately kept it from him because she didn't want him to have the same doubts. It was a heroic gift to him from the depths of her despair. But he had never realised that until now. Then, as Aunt

Meg's words sank in, his anguish started to lighten and his face glistened with a smile.

"Kieran, are you there? Are you there?" He could hear the anxiety even in Aunt Meg's dwarfed voice.

Lifting the phone back to his ear, he spoke with new confidence: "Yes, I'm still here. Mum was amazing, wasn't she? Totally amazing. I don't think I realised that until just now when it hit me what she went through — and Dad too."

He speculated that if his father had put his feelings into letters after Kathy's death, and if Kieran had those letters now, he would probably have discovered that his father's faith in God was as tortured as his mother's.

Aunt Meg agreed that the fatal accident was the biggest ever test of both his parents' religious convictions.

"But those letters and now this one … I've found out so much I didn't know. So much I wish I'd known when they were still alive. My eyes have finally opened."

The call ended with Kieran saying he wanted to talk some more about his mother's letter and Meg suggesting they meet for a drink the next evening.

"Best not to drown our sorrows in drink," he said. "How about you come over and I'll cook you a curry — I've got this fantastic recipe. Oh, and I'd like you to meet my girlfriend."

"You've got a girlfriend? You're a dark horse."

"Yes, I've not often felt that any girlfriend of mine would be good enough for my parents."

"But my standards aren't so exalted — is that what you're saying?"

She was teasing him but he was being serious.

"It's not that. I think this girl may be special and I don't want to hide her away. I've done too much of that sort of thing. Hiding my feelings, I mean."

After ending the call, Kieran sat for a long time thinking. Meg had argued in favour of blind faith. He had basically said it was too dangerous, taking such a risk with the unknown. That was why he didn't trust everything in the holy books. Now he wondered if the truth was that he'd simply been blind to faith and missed so much as a consequence.

And he said aloud to himself: "I've been blind to a lot of things."

FOUR VOTES OF THANKS

One may say thank you a thousand times while the heart remains thankless, ungrateful. Therefore, mere verbal thanksgiving is without effect. But real thankfulness is a cordial giving of thanks from the heart.

— 'Abdu'l-Bahá, The Promulgation of Universal Peace

THE CUSTOMER APPROACHED the counter slowly with a smile in his eyes. There was no swagger or intimidation. Here came a man relaxed and going at his own pace. There was no one else waiting to be served, so there was no need to rush anyway. The powerfully built, younger man behind the counter had a hint of a twinkle in his eye without looking directly at the approaching customer. An Indigenous assistant and a black American customer.

"G'day," the young assistant said quietly as a smile grew on his face.

Raising his free hand for a high five, the customer smiled back at the smile. "Brothers, man."

"Brothers," the assistant echoed in little more than a whisper as he hesitantly touched the raised hand. This wasn't in the customer relations manual.

"I want this book for my wife," the 30-something customer said, his smile now radiating beyond his face. "She's special, you know, and I want something special for her. I've got a feeling this is it."

He slapped the book down on the counter. The assistant looked at it, taking it in one hand and studying the face dominating the cover. "Archie Roach," the customer said. "I don't know him. I like that face though. Is he a good man? He looks like it."

"Yeah, I think so," the young assistant replied.

"He was one of the Stolen Generation, right?"

"Yeah, for sure. He's an inspiring guy."

"That's what I want to hear. This is his autobiography. Does your girl like him too?"

"She likes his music."

"But there's more to him than music?"

"Yeah."

"I want my wife to understand about this sort of stuff. Racism. She's not black but she's still real beautiful. I wanna paint her."

"Yeah? That's a cool thing to do. My girlfriend's not black either."

"And beautiful yeah?" The assistant nodded. "Paint her then and show her how beautiful she is."

"Oh, painting's not my thing."

"Just do it. I think the trick is to just let the brush find her." Another customer had moved up to the counter and was being served by a young woman. "That girl deserves to be painted too," the American said, looking at her. The assistant must have heard and she exchanged a surreptitious smile with her colleague but looked embarrassed.

"Well, I hope your wife enjoys Archie's story."

"She will. Tell me, brother, what's your name?"

"Troy."

"Good to meet you, Troy boy! It's the first time I've seen a black fella working in here."

"I'm a casual. I've only been here a couple of weeks. I'm at uni."

"Keep the flag flying, Troy boy. I'm Sam, short for Samir. That's 'Sam 'ere', not 'Sam here'."

As Troy laughed at his joke, Sam reached out a hand and squeezed Troy's dangling hand hard. Troy squeezed his only gently.

Troy rang up the sale and asked Sam to swipe his credit card.

"Black like us," Sam said over a lingering look at his credit card.

Troy slid the customer's purchase into a paper bag. "Thank you," he said with extra emphasis.

"No, I should thank you, bro. Thank you, thank you," he said, giving an exaggerated bow. "You treated me real good. It's not always like that in the shops."

"Oh, I know all about that kind of thing. Give your lady a hug from me."

Sam laughed. "I'll give her more than that, I promise you."

They looked at each other for a few seconds and as the customer started to walk away, he thrust a fist into the air behind him in acknowledgment of some special bond between the pair. The assistant shook his head, silently acknowledging to himself an unusual moment.

Troy said thank you to everyone he served but it was never as warmly offered or as warmly received as it was this time. The glow he was feeling temporarily washed away the stain that some customers left on him because of their obvious but unspoken dislike of being served by an Indigenous person. Customers who think all people like him go around robbing shops and stealing cars. It was racism, not so pure but very simple. But as he looked towards the next customer the glow faded.

She was a middle-aged woman and she was hesitating about coming to him at the counter. She was stealing glances at his white colleague, Serena, who hadn't yet finished serving her customer. He pretended not to notice and, smiling, called out: "Next please." She responded by slowly moving forward but not in the friendly manner of his previous customer. It was as unfriendly as a silent walk could be. Once at the counter, she didn't utter a single word to him as he served her. Instead of "thanks" when he handed back her loyalty card and book purchase, she took her silent displeasure with her and left gracelessly.

"Why do white people have so much trouble with black fellas?" he asks his girlfriend, Freya. She has gathered up her long, dark hair in a bun at the back of her head. They are in a restaurant waiting for the pizzas they have ordered. "I'm no threat. What are they frightened of?"

"They must be frightened you're going to have your wicked way with all the pretty white girls."

Troy quickly abandons his serious tone and joins in the joke. "If that's the case, you're brave taking me on because, as you know, I eat white chicks for dinner."

He hasn't told her yet about what happened on his way home that afternoon. He is thinking about telling her over pizza but he isn't sure if he should. How can he do it without coming across as some sort of hero? Freya runs her shoeless foot up his calf under the table but suddenly she's now the serious one as she smiles sweetly at him.

"I do know what it must be like for you and I think you handle all the racist crap brilliantly. I'm proud of you. I get some of that too when people find out I'm with you and it's obvious they don't approve. My uncle for one." She pauses and touches his hand across the table. "I love you."

He smiles and reaches out his right hand to stroke her cheek. She gently pulls it towards her lips and kisses it. How can he tell her after that? He's really not the saint she thinks he is and telling her about this afternoon will just strengthen the myth.

As he was walking to the bus station after completing his shift, he saw a drunken guy punching his girlfriend. She was yelling at him and not averse to retaliating but it was an uneven struggle. The young man was big and strong and clearly he meant to hurt her. Without hesitation, Troy ran towards them and thrust himself between them.

"Come on, man, it's not cool to hit a woman, back off," he said looking into the eyes of the assailant from a distance of about 5cm. He could smell the alcohol on his breath.

The man abused him ferociously with a spray of five swear words in one sentence, basically telling him that this was none of his business and the girl deserved a good beating for whatever it was that she'd done to him.

Troy managed to break the young man's grip on the girl and she backed away, leaving the two men to grapple with each other. Troy had him by the shoulders and was trying to push him away; the assailant had both his hands on Troy's head. The girl was hovering nearby and screaming at her attacker to stop. Then it was as if he had decided to take her advice. He let go of Troy and stepped back a pace.

"OK, that's good, man," Troy said. "Just stay calm. Leave this girl alone. Talk with her, man, don't hit her."

"I'm leaving her alone but I'm not leaving you alone, you friggin' mongrel."

With that, he pulled a small knife out of his jacket and waved it at Troy.

"No. Oh my God, Paul, don't do this," the girl yelled. "Are you mental?"

It wasn't the first time Troy had faced a knife, wasn't the first time he'd been in a fight. Although the knife gave the other guy a huge advantage, Troy was stone-cold sober and knew how to combat the knife. As a crowd of onlookers started to gather around them, he danced out of reach every time the knife was jabbed at him, biding his time before he could pounce. This went on for a couple of minutes with his attacker cranking up the threats of what he would do to him and the girl screaming over and over for him to stop.

Then one slash of the knife was too quick for him and caught Troy on the chest before he could dance out of the way. Blood seeped through his Black Lives Matter T-shirt.

The pizzas arrive and while Troy silently picks up a slice and starts eating, Freya just looks at hers as if in a trance. Then she lifts her gaze across the small table to her boyfriend.

"Is everything OK, Troy? You seem distracted."

"Do I? Sorry. No, it's all good," he lies.

"Did somebody give you a hard time at work today?"

"No."

"Sure?"

"Yes." He wants to tell her about the American customer as a way of showing her that it had been a good day, but Freya's questioning has irritated him and, raising his voice, he adds aggressively: "Now back off, will you?"

Freya is shocked to hear him suddenly turn on her. He isn't like that. Her face gives away her hurt and he can see it.

"No, I'm sorry. I shouldn't have said that, babe. I'm sorry."

He is a pitiful figure, staring sorrowfully at Freya as she finally picks up a slice of her pizza. She can see that he regrets snapping at her and yet the fact that he has done just that convinces her that something is up. Not being one to bypass issues, she changes her mind about eating the pizza, puts it back down and tries again.

"So you're definitely OK then? I got it all wrong when I said I thought something might be wrong?"

Troy winced, trying not to reveal that the cut was hurting him. He was disappointed with himself for not getting out of the way of the knife in time but it filled him with renewed determination to win this fight. He feinted to move one way and threw out a hand the other way, managing to grab the arm that held the knife in a vice-like grip. He quickly swayed back, elbowed his attacker hard in the stomach and, as the guy lost focus, he wrenched the knife free with his hand. He kicked it away and rammed home his advantage by wrapping one arm tightly around his neck and pinning one of his arms behind his back.

"Now apologise to this girl." Troy spat out the demand.

He refused so Troy tightened his grip on the young man's neck and he began to choke.

"OK, OK. Sorry."

Turning to the crowd, which had gathered and was now 15 or 20 strong, he shouted out for someone to call the police but as some spectators reached for their phones, two police cars screamed to a halt and four officers ran towards the men. Someone had already called the police. Troy released the young man for the police to deal with him, but instead they roughly yanked both men aside.

"This black animal attacked me. You gotta charge him with GBH," Paul shouted.

As the crowd started dispersing an elderly couple approached the police and the man, in red and blue flannel shirt and braces, gave Troy's assailant a withering look.

"Mate, he did no such thing. Officers, this man was attacking that girl over there." He pointed out the girl who didn't seem to know whether to approach or make a run for it. "This hero broke up the fight. He got this bloke off her but then this absolute moron pulled the knife on him. I'm ashamed to have the same colour skin as him. This Aboriginal lad did nothing wrong. He deserves a medal. I'll testify in court. Lock him up!"

The officers thanked him for explaining what had happened and the one holding Troy let him go. As he did so, he saw that there was blood on the sleeve of his uniform and that it came from Troy. By now there was a big red stain on Troy's shirt.

"You need to go to hospital, mate. I'll call for an ambulance."

Troy thanked him and sat down on a nearby bench to wait for the ambulance. The elderly couple approached and stood over him. The man's wife commended him for his bravery.

"That poor girl could have been killed or seriously injured if not for you," she said. "Thank you. Very few men would have done what you've just done, putting your life on the line like that."

"Yes, I want to thank you too," her husband said. "You're a very special person. I hope your wife appreciates you."

"Yes, if you've got a wife! Don't embarrass the boy, you old fool! If you have a wife or girlfriend though, I hope she knows how lucky she is."

Troy smiled, lost for words. It felt to him that their expressions of thanks were mined from much deeper down than the standard, albeit sincere, thanks he gave customers in the bookshop. As he looked away a little embarrassed, he spotted the girl still hovering uncertainly. She gave him a quick, nervous smile. She looked no more than about 17 or 18 and probably didn't have the confidence to come over and put her gratitude into words. Her smile was her unspoken thanks and it was as meaningful for Troy as the couple's.

Troy called out to one of the police officers: "Make sure that girl over there is OK. She might need some treatment too because he was beating the crap out of her."

"Yes, Freya, you got it wrong. Your pizza's going cold."

He shoots her a reassuring smile and she smiles back. But as he eats and Freya chats — Freya can talk all day given half a chance — he thinks about that old couple and the girl. They were all so grateful to him. They spoke from the heart in their own ways. Then there were those comments about his "wife". He'll save telling Freya about that for another day. Nor has he forgotten the American with the Archie Roach book. He isn't used to having so many people thanking him big time like that in just one day.

"Are you listening to me?" Freya asks, jolting him back to the table.

"Yes, of course."

"So, what's your answer?"

"Answer to what?"

"Troy, you're hopeless! I asked what that bulge was under your jacket? And why are you even wearing a jacket on a warm night like this? I was wondering if you'd hurt yourself and had some sort of dressing."

"It's nothing really."

"That tells me it's certainly not 'nothing'. Fess up."

He looks at her but doesn't say anything. She disarms him with a wide-eyed look that has him cornered. He sighs heavily. Freya runs marathons and is treating this discussion like one of her runs. She's full of gritty determination.

"You don't give up, do you?"

"No, I don't. Runners never give up. What's happened? I'll keep asking until you tell me."

"OK, OK, you win. I intervened in a fight. It was nothing. It was all over in seconds."

"See, that wasn't so hard, was it? Now I want the unsanitised version of what happened."

CONSUMED BY FIRE

*The tongue is a smouldering fire, and
excess of speech a deadly poison. Material
fire consumeth the body, whereas the fire
of the tongue devoureth both heart and
soul. The force of the former lasteth but
for a time, whilst the effects of the latter
endureth a century.*

— Baha'u'llah, Gleanings

"ANY OF YOU seen John lately?" one of the men asked. "I haven't
seen hide nor hair of him for ages."

"I think his wife's left him," another said.

"Really? He should be out celebrating," a third member of
the group said.

"Why's that?"

"Oh, she's nothing but trouble."

Another explained: "She can't keep her eyes off other wom-
en's husbands."

"You blokes are speaking from personal experience?"

"Well, no, but – "

"I heard she came on to Warren who used to live over the road a couple of years ago."

"She did?"

"I think the old grandpa quite enjoyed the attention!"

"He probably didn't exactly discourage her."

"Course not. Would you?"

The four men laughed loudly. A fifth smiled politely, choosing not to risk alienating himself by expressing any disquiet about the conversation. Like sitting in a friend's garden without making any comment about how he'd let the weeds get out of hand and ruin everything. Silence — politeness — can be a cop-out but it's a way of keeping the peace. Especially when the others in the conversation are all white Australians and you're not. Even though he was born to Vietnamese parents in Australia, he knew this group of neighbours saw him as "different". Not one of them.

The barbecue chat moved on to topical news items — the TV presenter who committed suicide after being hit by a tsunami of online abuse; the summer of horrendous bushfires, the coronavirus pandemic and the mother and her children who were set on fire in their car and died horrible deaths.

The TV presenter had been a prolific Instagram user so one of the men proffered: "Those who live by the sword may, and do, die by the sword — not that I'm condoning trolls, but people like this woman invite attention from the unhinged."

The bushfires happened, as another of them put it: "Not because of climate change but because of kowtowing to the greens by federal and state governments — that Greens leader is an idiot".

Coronavirus, it was said, "predictably originated in China like all the other pandemics — I've never liked the Chinese, friggin' shifty lot. No offence, Anh."

They at least agreed it was unforgivable that the husband set fire to his wife and kids but there was a voice of caution: "No one ever looks at the behaviour of women in driving men to do these terrible sorts of things — but you daren't say that these days."

Throughout these conversations, the fifth man was either silent or his views were quietly at odds with the others'. When he suggested that whatever the provocation, if indeed there was any, it was wrong for a man to try and resolve a problem by violence, everyone agreed but even then one of the others tried to turn it into a joke: "There are plenty of women who'd win any physical fight with one of us!"

Inside, sitting around the kitchen bench, a group of wives and a couple of their partners were chatting too. They dissected the latest episode of Married at First Sight and readily accepted the program's invitation to look for the worst in the various competitors. They had differing views about who was the sluttiest and who was the biggest cheat.

Then the conversation turned to movies they had seen recently and the two who had seen Little Women agreed that it was one of the year's best movies. Another, who wanted to see it but hadn't, blamed her husband for refusing to go. "He never goes to any movies that I want to see." Opinion was split on A Beautiful Day in the Neighbourhood, which was about an "impossibly nice" children's TV presenter. One of the women thought the character was "boring" and the movie would appeal only to bored people; another thought the character was "inspirational" and the movie should be made compulsory viewing for all men.

One of the group, Josephine, a Malaysian, spoke quietly as "one of your bored people" (they laughed awkwardly). Pointing out that the character had summarised his philosophy as "be kind, be kind, be kind", she talked about how refreshing that was because there was so little kindness in the world. She blamed the media, social media in particular, and reality TV shows for "stoking the fires of anger, disrespect, intolerance and hatred".

"Oh, for heaven's sake, lighten up, love," said one of the other women. "No one takes reality TV seriously. It's just a bit of fun. And there are lots of people in this world who don't deserve to be treated kindly."

Josephine and Anh were the first to leave. They both felt bruised by the conversations at their neighbours' barbecue. They had lived in the street for four years and this was the third get-together they'd attended with this group, so they knew they were out of kilter with the street's prevailing wisdom on most subjects and tried not to alienate them by quibbling aggressively. They conceded that they liked some of the neighbours, particularly an Afghani refugee couple, a Japanese woman and an environmental scientist, and they also identified neighbours with the most poisonous tongues.

"So how was the barbie at Tom and Jerry's — I mean Tim and Geraldine's?" their 16-year-old daughter, Gabby, asked as she bounded in from a friend's house a few doors away.

"Awful," Anh replied. "Your mother and I have compared notes and haven't been able to find any redeeming features about the conversations we had there."

"Well, did you at least enjoy the food?"

"That was actually quite good," Josephine said. "I was pleasantly surprised that there were some vegetarian things apart from mine."

"So it wasn't all bad then, parentals?"

"Yes, but they're so negative and racist too," Anh said. "One guy didn't like the Chinese because they're 'shifty'."

"Really?" said Josephine. "Does that include Malaysians?"

"The bushfires were greenies' fault and women were to blame for their husbands killing them. Give me strength."

Like most young people, Gabby was permanently attached to her smartphone and she was busily tapping away at it.

"Are your ageing parents boring you again?" Josephine asked with a twinkle in her eye as the conversation stalled.

"No, not at all. I'm looking for something I read the other day and I reckon you should share this with our neighbours. By the way, as you well know, my friend Olivia's parents were at that barbie and she's lovely. Found it! Listen to this, parentals, this is the quote: *'The tongue is a smouldering fire and excess of speech a deadly poison. Material fire consumeth the body, whereas the fire of the tongue devoureth both heart and soul. The force of the former lasteth but for a time, whilst the effects of the latter endureth a century.'* Do you like it? Out of the mouths of babes and all that."

"Thanks, daughter, that's all very nice," Anh said. "I used to think in black and white like that when I was your age. But life's not that simple."

"It IS that simple, Dad! What's hard is to stop being so cynical, then aiming much higher and really going for it."

Anh was bristling and about to pick a fight with Gabby. Josephine the peacemaker got there first.

"Gabby, dear, what would you like for dinner?"

"I don't suppose you'd want to fire up the barbie, would you?!"

SEPARATE TABLES

*A new life is, in this age, stirring within all
the peoples of the earth; and yet none hath
discovered its cause or perceived its motive ...*
— Baha'u'llah, Gleanings

THE SUN SHONE to order on this spring morning. The two friends swooned in the welcome embrace of a feathery breeze. The river at the café's edge sparkled with new life. About a kilometre downriver trucks could be seen, but not heard, gliding silently across a bridge to the port. Occasional boats, palaces on water, floated past. The café owners had slid back big floor-to-ceiling windows, opening it up to both the river and a children's play area, where mums were on guard armed with takeaway coffees and smartphones. And the intoxicating aroma of coffee weaved tantalisingly across every table, inside and out, at the cafe. Today the city felt excitingly different. This was surely the perfect day and the perfect place. A scene from a tourism video.

But the two men at an outside table were talking about our imperfect world and how badly it was going. Really badly.

In the space of 90 minutes and two coffees each, they skimmed across the war in Syria, tax avoidance, the paralysing power of party politics, the relentless assault on fish stocks, countries' refusal to abide by international treaties, rorts, ethical failings ...

And all the while the world smiled benignly on everyone at the river's edge. Even the river beamed with contentment.

That was the problem. Despite the world's gathering storm, life here in Perth looked unassailable. Fabulous weather, great cafe, nice people, beautiful waitress, everyone seemingly comfortable enough. Plenty to keep the locals buoyant, a safe distance from the storm, but they were deluding themselves.

Even in this one city, as close as any modern city gets to paradise, there were thousands of people who were miserable. People wanting answers. Their hopes in tatters; life without purpose. Despite being close at hand, these people were as invisible as the untold millions going through great traumas all over the world. Refugees stranded between uncertain freedom and persecution; ethnic or religious minorities targeted by draconian regimes; flood victims whose homes had been washed away; families grieving over the loss of loved ones in a mass shooting.

There was a world of pain on an horrific scale out beyond the deceptive serenity of this very civilised, well-ordered and polite cafe society. But what could anyone here possibly do about such overwhelming problems? Best then to retreat into looking after No.1. Survival of the fittest was the name of the game; turning a deaf ear to others' problems and instead choosing self-preservation. Best not to interfere in other people's business.

As the two men really got into the problems of the world, they ordered their second coffees to fuel their thinking. As is often the way when people discuss such matters, religion became the focus.

After all, they were both religious, shared the same faith and were fatigued from encounters with people who had no time for any kind of religion. They could understand why people were like that. Religion was behind a lot of the world's problems. But for them, a lot of so-called "religion" bore little resemblance to what they understood as religion. Muslims and Christians believed in the one same God, so why would they kill each other? Catholics and Protestants hated each other but they were all Christians. Priests abused children in their care even though they knew their church regarded it as a sin and punishable by God. No wonder people treated religion with disdain, even though, strangely, many sent their children to church-owned schools.

Whatever way the men looked at it, they saw the old order as being in danger of collapse. The world was falling apart and no one in power showed any sign of being able to stop the rot. That was exactly what their faith had predicted almost 200 years ago, along with a plan to turn everything around. Now, although disintegration was clear for everyone to see, people were not taking heed of the warning ripples; not curious for answers. Time and time again the pair found friends and colleagues just switched off when they tried talking to them about their faith. Both men had answers! They knew a way through the mess! Yet no one wanted to hear about it, they lamented.

But at the table next to them there was a middle-aged woman sitting on her own and eavesdropping on their conversation. Her floral dress was crumpled from several days' continuous wear. She was thinking the men sounded different and was impressed that they had forsaken idle chit-chat for weightier subjects. She would have liked to join in. She too was puzzled by religion but hadn't given up on it. With last month's diagnosis shortening her life to maybe just another year, she was desperate to find a lifeboat that could rescue her. But she didn't like to intrude and so she did no more than listen.

On another outside table, there was a businessman pretending to be interested in his colleague's rant about the latest footy scandal. Under the table his right foot was tapping furiously while his face had dropped anchor looking hard at his companion with a fixed stare. He hated footy. He hated all sport but the religion of Aussie mateship wouldn't allow him to openly admit it. He watched the sports news on TV only so he could sound credible in conversations such as these. What he would have given to be sharing his table with someone who had no interest in sport. Everything in his life was so shallow.

An Indigenous elder with two of his family at another table surveyed the scene inside the café and thought to himself that probably no one there had an Indigenous friend or even liked Indigenous people. The three of them were talking loudly and he could feel the whole café looking at the three of them as if they were intruders. This was probably a roomful of pampered white people who didn't have a clue what it was like to cop racial abuse every day. He saw that there were one or two exceptions — a young African mum was at a table with some other white mums and their babies and there was also an elderly Asian couple. He wondered if any of them would have understood why he was so angry.

Sitting at a big round table in the far corner of the cafe, a mother laughed with a group of other mums. Last night she took a whack in the face from her husband and she was choosing not to tell anyone or to do anything about it. She was trying to put on a brave face.

An old man sat at another inside table with his middle-aged daughter. His walker was abandoned nearby between his table and another, making it almost impossible for anyone to edge past it. He could no longer go anywhere on his own, either walking or driving. His body was failing him. He saw no hope, no reason to keep on living. Everyone was avoiding him. Even his daughter gave the impression that these weekly outings were a burden for her.

Back outside at another table, a young woman in her running gear was talking anxiously on the phone to her boyfriend. She was trapped in a relationship that was going nowhere. He was married and even though he had again told her he loved her, he said he couldn't leave his wife. She would never be anything but his secret mistress.

Wreckage at every table. Comfort and hope in short supply. They were all aching silently; desperate to find a way through the wreckage. But no one made a move. All were strangers to each other, sitting at separate tables. Coffee anyone?

OPEN BOOK

Dispel my grief by Thy bounty and Thy
generosity, O God, my God, and banish
mine anguish through Thy sovereignty
and Thy might.

— Bahá'u'lláh, Prayers

I'M ON THE shelf again. I've been here lots of times. Waiting to
be noticed and taken out. I really need to be out where people can
see me but here it's dark and it's easy to get forgotten. For someone
to find me here, they've really got to be persistent. Or desperate.
But that's OK. You could say this is a sad story and although I've
turned my back on the world in some ways, I'm actually not sad at
all. I believe that God will lead the right person to me. I don't need
to go out of my way to be noticed. That's because God and I are
closely connected. We have an unbreakable bond. It's not that I'm
some kind of prophet or guru but I can definitely feel God guiding
me in what I say. Oh, I suppose that sounds arrogant. Is it really
arrogant to sense the presence of God? Many people are blind to

spiritual forces. Ha, they can't believe what they can't see. And if people think I sound like I'm talking myself up as a prophet, well, I'm not all that special. There are thousands — no, millions — like me. But I can be special to a person who takes me by the hand and gets me. They rely on me, that one person. Eventually, they move on. By then I've helped them through their particular problem and my job is probably done, although sometimes spending time with me doesn't work out the way they'd hoped and they take it out on me. I think it's their ego getting in the way. It happened to me the other day.

I'd been with this beautiful soul. She was in a lot of pain. Her parents and sister had died in a car accident that wasn't their fault. It was a drunk driver. She was devastated. Understandably, I guess, she was looking for comfort and so she turned to me. Someone had told her that I had special powers that would help her. We talked for hours, through her tears and her anger, and I thought I was helping her see some light at the end of the tunnel. So it was a great shock to me when she turned against me. She slammed me into a wall and shouted at me: "You've got no idea what I'm going through. If you did, you'd bring my parents and my sister back to me. How could you let this happen?"

To say the least, she was expecting a lot of me. I can't perform miracles; they are scientifically impossible. But I guess this sort of thing happens a lot when good people have suffered a deep trauma and they blame God for letting such a terrible thing happen. I did explain to her that God is immeasurably beyond our comprehension and that we just need to trust Him, but that's a hard one when He appears to have deserted them and taken loved ones away from them so cruelly.

I can talk in words but somehow people have to transcend the limitation of words. Words and sentences are like doors that we can choose to open and go through or just walk past. But where they go if they manage to open that door is up to them, not me. Words are not some wonder medicine — take twice a day and you will instantly be cured. Perhaps we have grown too used to living in a world of instant gratification. You want something and you want it now — gimme, gimme, gimme. When a person applies that kind of thinking to the realm of spirituality, they are probably not going to get the answer they're looking for. God often seems to be ignoring their pleas or just responding with ideas they don't want to hear.

And that's when I get dumped and end up back on the shelf. When it seems prayers haven't been answered, I often get dumped as if it's all my fault. It's rude but I understand their frustration. I get what they're going through but it's painful for me too, you know. Sometimes I'm battered and bruised from being with them in their darkest moments. They blame me, call me useless.

Of course, I would prefer being with someone who loves seeing me, whom I manage to inspire and who takes me with them everywhere they go. But my heart also goes out to those who have lost a loved one or who are experiencing a terrible personal crisis and direct their anger at me. I can absorb their pain like a sponge and give out to them. That's what I am known for.

Where I live, there are a lot of people buzzing around and sometimes, when no one has time to stop and talk with me, it's frustrating. It's as if I'm hiding in plain sight. And now time is taking a toll. My edges are not as sharp as they used to be; I'm getting a little ragged. What I'm really saying is that I'm getting old but many of those who come to me seem comforted by the fact that I have obviously been through a lot and my words are seen as all the more valuable as a result. Age-old wisdom, one young person called it, as he introduced me to his friend. The friend said that such wisdom might have worked in times past but old ideas didn't work in today's world where attitudes and beliefs have changed. It's disappointing to hear people talk like that. Too many these days form their opinions without really investigating or knowing the full story and they refuse to let anyone or anything uncouple them from their prematurely formed opinions.

What they're doing is judging a book just by looking at its cover. They don't feel the need to open the book and read what's inside. I blame social media for a lot of that kind of instant judgment. Prejudice is even more of a factor, whether it is handed down from possibly several generations of a person's family or simply a new prejudice created through ill-informed media and gossip. But I have faith that there will always be a place for me. I will always have friends.

FEAST OUT OF FAMINE

Increase their sincerity, so that with all
humility and contrition they may turn to Thy
kingdom and be occupied with service to the
world of humanity. May each one become
a radiant candle. May each one become a
brilliant star. May each one become beautiful
in colour and redolent of fragrance in the
kingdom of God.
— 'Abdu'l-Bahá, The Promulgation of Universal Peace

WANDERING LONELY AS A CLOUD

IT WAS ONE of those still, sunny days when life actually seems worthwhile. For the first time since the first shoots of spring three weeks earlier, he had discarded the anorak in which he'd hibernated all winter and instead gone out in shirtsleeves. No hat, even though his wife always insisted he wear one. The sky was a dazzling blue, just one small puff of cloud, and if the forecast was correct, the temperature was climbing up to 27 Celsius. Days like this were his favourite time of the year. Nicely warm, not sweaty-hot as in January, and no rain or ice-tinged wind.

He was wandering the city alone for the day. Bus to Canning Bridge train station next to the Swan River, down the steps to the platform, swipe his Smart Rider card and on a train to the city two stops away. On the bus, he had absorbed himself in a novel by an Indigenous writer about an Indigenous mother and adult daughter going on a literary tour of England. In organising this, the daughter hoped that it would bring them closer together, and it did. It was a book full of hope for a family torn apart by tragedy. Not only that but the tour, as described in the book, went to places that he and his wife had visited so happily more than 10 years earlier. It took him back there; brought him back together with her. That's why he bought it on impulse after seeing the blurb on the back of the book.

"Look, Jane Austen's buried here. I never knew that, did you? But the inscription doesn't say anything about her achievements as a writer. I wonder what will be written on my tombstone. 'She kept her husband on the straight and narrow'"?!

Although there were a few empty seats on the train, including "priority seats" for old fogies like him, he chose to stand. He didn't want to surrender to old age. The view out the window was of the sparkling Swan River stretched languidly beneath the occasional small cloud in the blue sky. An excited young boy climbed like a monkey up a pole in the middle of the carriage and touched the roof. The child then demanded, but didn't get, his disinterested mother's praise. He felt sorry for the child and offered him a compensatory smile and a "wish I could do that". Immediately, he regretted it. People were so suspicious these days of strangers talking to a child. But no one looked up from their mobile phones.

It saddened him that people were always preoccupied with whatever was on their phones. He had had a mobile for about 20 years and he was carrying his latest one with him today in his pocket but he hadn't looked at it once since leaving home more than half an hour ago. The phone-addicted passengers were missing a treat out the window and a treat inside the carriage with this young chap doing his monkey impression. Still, as long as they weren't doing him any harm, why should he get steamed up about modern lifestyles? Especially on such a perfect day as this.

In the city, his priority was to find a café where he could enjoy his daily coffee, a long black topped up. The small café he chose in the heart of the business district — once such a familiar domain but not these days — was busy, although it was mostly serving take-aways and only two other tables were occupied. At both of them young men in suits sat armed and preoccupied with their smart-phones. Some discordant noise oozed through the coffee-scented air. It wasn't music to his 20th-century ears. When one pair got up to leave, he noticed that their suit jackets were short and tight, like their pants. He remembered wearing more generous amounts of cloth when he worked in the city. He returned to his book and when he next looked up, he was alone in the café. Alone again, naturally. Wasn't that the title of an old pop song?

Pulling his small backpack onto his shoulder, he left and headed for the shops. A homeless man was stretched out asleep on a bench in a small patch of park guarded by tall office buildings. Like speck of dirt in a cup of coffee. He wandered into Dymocks bookshop, where he studied the display of bestsellers. None of these books interested him. He asked for a book by a

British palliative care doctor he'd seen on television the previous evening but it wasn't in stock. Maybe that was for the best. It might have been painful to revisit palliative care, impressive though the author was on TV.

Leaving Dymocks and walking along the Hay Street Mall, he remembered once he and his wife saw a human statue come to life here and scare a child who had been looking at "it". Everyone passing at the time had laughed. Nothing to laugh about today. He cut through an arcade to the Myer department store on the other side of a pedestrian mall. He entered through the obligatory battery of beauty products and assistants — mostly women and one or two who looked like men but he couldn't be sure. They waited, ready to swoop on any sign of prey. He was of no interest to them. Too old, not the right gender. His wife had always looked for the Clinique counter and when he spotted it on his way through this time, he felt a shudder and quickened his pace.

He was headed downstairs to the men's department. He needed a new short-sleeved shirt for summer. It was going to be his first summer without her. How often he and his wife had come to this Myer store and while she looked for dresses or yet more anti-ageing products, he left her to it and went downstairs. Invariably, they would reunite — he only occasionally with a purchase and she easily outspending him. He would tease her over that.

"Surely by now you've already eradicated every known wrinkle — at great expense, too. We won't be able to afford to eat tonight!"

He now realised in hindsight that sometimes he went too far with teasing her. This time, as always, there were a lot of special offers downstairs but nothing special took his fancy, and his wife wasn't waiting for him upstairs. No one to tease today.

The Japanese chain, Uniqlo, now had a shop in Perth and it was taking customers away from traditional department stores. He and his wife quite liked Uniqlo. He remembered how they'd bought up big at Uniqlo in London's West End a few years earlier. Walking across the mall towards the store, he passed a young man yelling a stream of obscenities at a young woman who was, presumably, his girlfriend. He hoped she had the courage and strength to sever the tentacles that had her in their grip.

In Uniqlo he found a couple of shirts that he liked. They weren't his usual bland blue or brown but had vibrant patterns — one a red and yellow check. His wife had always encouraged him to be bolder in his fashion choices but he had always erred on the side of conservatism, sticking to tried and trusted looks. Strange now, he thought to himself, how he was finally taking her advice.

At the place where you paid, there was a queue of customers waiting to complete their purchases. When he got to the front of the queue, he discovered that there was no one to serve him. Instead, there were a series of stations with machines at which to swipe credit cards — but no humans. He was flummoxed and couldn't work out what he needed to do. Spotting his confusion, a young Japanese assistant approached from behind. She gently explained that he just had to put the two shirts into the receptacle at one of the stations. Then the amount owing would automatically come up on the credit card machine. She smiled warmly and he smiled back. It was refreshing to be served by such a polite and strikingly beautiful young woman, even though she wasn't actually serving him in the normal meaning of the word. Instead, she was showing him how to serve himself. He thanked her and said it was a shame the system had been changed. "It's so much nicer to deal with a human rather than an automated machine," he said. She smiled sympathetically.

As she moved off to help another customer, he thought to himself that if only he were 40 or 50 years younger, he would ask her out. That reminded him of how his wife always noticed when an attractive woman caught his eye.

"She's pretty, isn't she? Young enough to be your granddaughter."

It was starting to get busy around the city centre. Lunchtime was looming. Invasion of the suits. He had no appetite for going to any more shops. Did any man? Instead he decided to go to the State Library. He needed its silence and stillness. It was a place he came to occasionally on his own when he'd retired and his wife was still alive. It had struck him then that it was a place of escape; somewhere that let its occupants take refuge from the world. Not that he really needed refuge back then, but he liked his own company; liked being in the company of books. Did he still enjoy his own company? His permanently heavy heart was a lot to carry around alone every day.

The library was on the other side of the city train station. There was an elevated walkway between the big open area of Forrest Place and the Myer store. It connected with a bridge across busy Wellington Street into the station. To his left, there were steps and escalators down to the various platforms. On both sides, there were stalls selling drinks and takeaway food, newspapers and magazines. On his right, there were empty shops. He remembered there used to be a good bookshop but it was gone, like so many other shops in cities everywhere.

Emerging from the station, still on a now-wider, open-air elevated passage, he crossed Roe Street, most of which had been dug up for some reason. To his right was the Art Gallery of WA, currently closed for the building of a new rooftop area. Why would an art gallery want a rooftop area, he wondered? Perhaps paintings alone were no longer sufficiently interesting to attract patrons. Moments later, past a couple of pop-up coffee shops, a large ragtag group of primary schoolchildren in green uniforms was making its way in his direction. They'd left the new home of the West Australian Museum, which loomed large on the right. Three teachers and presumably parent helpers herded the children unobtrusively, seemingly happy for the group to be chatting and laughing without paying much attention to where they were walking. A pair of boys clearly pre-programmed to be mischievous, suddenly appeared almost under his feet as one chased the other. He had to stop or else he would have collided with them. He remembered school visits from his own childhood being strictly marshalled in a line, with definitely no talking and no leaving the line. Of course, he never went on school excursions with his daughters — he was always at work and his wife would go when she could.

Once he had navigated his way past the school group, the State Library was directly in front of him. It was a five-storey building dominated by horizontal lines of blank glass and devoid of any curves or embellishment other than a receding effect as each of the top three storeys was set back slightly from the one below. Nothing like some of the fine ornate buildings he knew that housed public libraries. At less than 40 years of age, this building already seemed weary. Still, at least its silent stillness would be a welcome escape from the burbling sea of city noise. A weary home for a weary walker.

He headed for a large area to the left of the entrance foyer, where he could sit at a desk or table or a soft bench seat and immerse himself in his book. But, as he entered, he noticed an exhibition in the far corner. Prize-winning press photographs from the previous year were on display. So many of the images depicted life in war zones and the aftermath of natural disasters. They demanded his attention. He viewed most of the photographs and read their captions. He saw haunted faces, impoverishment, desolation and hopelessness. Much of it was from Third World countries and it was all captured in the sophisticated lenses of expensive First World cameras. It was a world he had never experienced, having successfully avoided any war or natural disaster. He had so much to be thankful for and yet he was downcast, even before these images burned themselves into his mind.

Eventually, with a sigh, he left the exhibition and found a seat at a table a safe distance from anyone else. That "anyone" included two or three dishevelled homeless men sprawled out on benches, a tell-tale bag of paltry belongings on the floor beside one of them a humiliating status symbol. After surveying the thinly populated scene — mostly just young students — he took off his backpack and got out his book. At first, he found it hard to make sense of the words on the page because images from the exhibition were holding his thoughts hostage. The first page was very slow going but gradually he managed to speed up as the images slowly released their grip.

Pausing at the end of a chapter and trying to get a feel for the literary journey of the book's characters through the eyes and ears of both the mother and the daughter, he wondered whether he should have opted for something lighter like the page-turner he'd finished earlier that week. Yet he struggled to accept that stimulation generated by either type of book could do much to help him wrench himself free of his suffocating grief.

THE MAN IN A HAT

READING HIS BOOK, he didn't hear the footsteps approaching behind him. When a voice jovially inquired if it was a good book, he looked up with a startled expression. "I hope I didn't give you a fright," said a well-built man about his age in an Akubra hat, flannel shirt and jeans that had seen better days. Now relieved to discover that he wasn't under attack, he held up his book to show the intruder the title, After Story, by Larissa Behrendt.

"I've not heard of that one." Then Mr Akubra read aloud the endorsement underneath the title, "'A moving story of going far away to find home again — a beautiful, hopeful book.' Sounds more worthwhile than the kind of book I read. My last one was by Henning Mankell but it was just one of those airport books. The sort you forget almost the moment you finish the last page. Have you ever read any of his?"

This interruption was irritating and he replied with a deliberate lack of enthusiasm: "No, I've never heard of him."

"You really should try and make more effort to be polite, you know, even when someone's irritating you."

Far from taking the hint, the man sat down uncomfortably close to him, clearly intent on further conversation. "Fair enough. The book was far too long." He got no response but was visibly at ease as he removed his hat, scratched at his thinning head of grey hair and stretched out his legs.

Undeterred, the newly installed pest asked what brought him there today with his "book of hope". That was an invitation to open up a much more difficult book, the story of life after the death of his wife; how lost he was and how much he was struggling. But this was an irritating stranger, albeit a 70-ish man like him in a red and blue check shirt that was definitely less impressive than his Uniqlo purchase. It was ridiculous to even think of baring his soul to him. So he took a safe option and said he was just having a break from the shops — looking for some peace and quiet, a less than subtle hint that this conversation wasn't welcome. He stopped short of telling him outright to go away and bother somebody else. Surely his words sent enough of a signal to this man. But still, he didn't take the hint.

"I try and avoid the shops. I often come up to town and find something interesting to read in here. There's often gold hidden away in this library. Not literally of course. I meet some interesting folks in here. Everyone's got a story; everyone's on the run from something."

If this intruder refused to leave him in peace, he would give him a hard time instead. It was far too much of a sweeping generalisation to say that everyone in this library was on the run from something. So he asked what about the many students who came here to write their essays or swot for exams — surely they weren't trying to escape from anything?

"Good question. Sure, they don't talk so readily but I reckon they're on the run from letting themselves go. They're frightened about what exam failure will mean and so they try to block out everything else young people like them should be doing."

So he understood a generation more than 50 years younger than his? Mr Nuisance was out of his depth. "That's only your perspective. At our sort of age, it's ridiculous to think we can claim to understand young people."

The man smiled. Despite the resistance, he was getting him to engage; bringing him out of himself and his book. This was familiar territory.

"I made sure my son didn't spend his whole childhood buried in schoolwork," the man persisted. "I encouraged him to be outdoors like a real Aussie playing sport, being with his friends, discovering new places. He wasn't a straight-A student but he did OK and he has a good life now. Have you got kids?"

"Yes, two daughters, one here in Perth and the other in Melbourne."

Jasmine, in Melbourne, was with a partner but had no children and Jade, in Perth, was unhappily single as of last week. Jade had been in a long-term relationship with Joshua. He was already married when they first met and his dalliance with Jade ended the marriage. Like her sister, Jade had never married but she and Joshua were together for eight years and had a child, Jacob, who was now three. Jade, Josh and Jacob — the Triple J family, as he called them. Only now it was just Double J. Jade's parents never really took to Josh. In particular, her late mother, Greta, saw the affair and break-up of Josh's marriage as a big red light.

"A man who cheats on his wife will more than likely cheat on the next one. I'm afraid Jade's always been attracted to the wrong sort."

Now Josh had done just as Greta feared. It was yet another reason to feel sad, as if he didn't have enough sadness already in his life. Jade needed her mother more than ever and she wasn't here for her anymore. He was a poor substitute for his wife. It was yet another blow.

"Jade, in Perth, has our only grandchild but she's just broken up with her partner after many years together."

"Gee, that's tough. Has she been crying on your shoulder? I bet she has."

The question was another invitation to relax his defences and this time he did, but cautiously: "Yes, she's been very teary."

"Daughters have a special relationship with their fathers. "Are you and your daughter close? Or is she a mummy's girl?"

He hesitated about answering. If he said his wife died just three months ago, there would be more questions. Did he really want to get into that sort of conversation in this public place with a complete stranger? No, he didn't even know his name or anything about him. Yet, at the same time, he knew that he needed to talk to someone about Greta. He was bottling up everything, even with his two daughters. He was keeping his emotions in cold storage, the place where he usually kept them out of harm's way, and now Jade's new all-consuming crisis ruled out any opportunity to open up to her. She was now the one in crisis, not him. It was exhausting dealing with grief and loss, whether it be death or relationship break-up; yet exhausting not dealing with these things.

"I get on well with both my daughters but I struggle to talk with them about their love lives. Then, again," he added as if talking to himself, "that's more my wife's area of expertise."

Like a flash, the interloper struck. "So do they talk to your wife about that?"

Oh dear, he left himself open to this. Now he would have to tell him that Greta was dead. There was no escape, not even in the State Library, where he hoped to find respite. "They did but my wife's not with us anymore." No, that was a mistake. He made it sound like they were divorced. "I mean, she passed away a few months ago," he added awkwardly.

The man knew it! He knew from his body language, the squirming and wringing of his hands, that he was hiding something bigger than his daughter's break-up. He wanted him to talk about it but first he wanted to warm up the conversation by getting it on first-name terms.

"What was her name? And talking of names, what's yours? I'm Zach, by the way."

"Greta. Her name was Greta. I met her at school, 55 years ago."

"Well done, you two. Not many couples make it that far down the road. You must miss her terribly."

Suddenly, Greta was standing in front of him, looking at him with that coy grin that encouraged him to sit next to her on the bus to school one morning. She was having the same effect on him again.

Every morning she was there at the back of the bus with her friends. They were at different schools and he only ever saw her on the bus. Green blazer, check skirt, white socks. A brunette with shoulder-length hair and a lovely smile. In fact, she seemed to be smiling most of the time on the bus. Even today when she was on her own.

"On your own today? What's happened to your friends?"

"Oh, I do travel unsupervised occasionally, you know."

Her smile had deepened.

"Well, that does leave you open to unwelcome attention from boys like me."

Oh no, he sounded like a pervert.

"I think I can cope with it."

"Could we meet after school one day? Like tomorrow?"

She looked at him intently. Her smile was undimmed. He
so wanted her to say yes. Say yes. Please.

"What's your name?"

"Clem. You?"

Just say yes.

"Greta. Nice to meet you, Clem."

She held out her hand for him to shake it, which he did.

"So, Clem, where will I find you tomorrow after school?"

Boy, she was so lovely. And he was so lucky that she liked him. Yet there was no way of avoiding the painful truth. There came a time when he grew tired of that smile and her relentless loyalty. He betrayed her but she forgave him. How he hated what he'd done.

"Oh my God, you're a lucky guy to have found love for life at such a young age."

"Yes, I certainly was lucky. I was blessed but I was never the husband she deserved."

"That's your grief talking, my friend. My friend without a name!"

He was lost in his memories, staring at his 15-year-old girlfriend and wishing he could start over with her. Two kids on a bus who had never spoken before, blissfully unaware of future pitfalls. He smiled distractedly and said his name was Clem. Zach immediately began singing quietly: "Oranges and lemons, say the bells of St Clement's."

Clem turned from his school sweetheart and looked at Zach. "My mother used to sing that song to me when I was a kid. She was the only one who ever called me Clement rather than just Clem."

Now Zach had not just unlocked the door but opened it wide and Clem was venturing through it.

"These past three months since Greta died, I've really been wallowing in my memories, seeing my mistakes. Things I should have done but didn't, and feeling like I thoroughly deserve the punishment I'm suffering."

"That's your grief talking again, Clem. Those black clouds will blow over in time."

"Will they? I don't think I will ever be happy again."

Then an older couple walked past and the man, whose violently colourful Hawaian shirt was at odds with his shuffling gait, threw a loud "Buongiorno!" in their direction. He smiled eagerly at them. Zach matched his smile and responded with two thumbs up. Then, without stopping to talk, the man waved a hand in farewell and in the same booming voice said: "Arrivederci".

Zach slapped Clem on the back and, completely ignoring the interruption, told him that he might be in a dark place at the moment but it wouldn't crush him. He was inevitably dwelling on the past but gradually he would start to look to the future.

"The thing is," Clem said, "I never really prepared for this. Being alone, I mean, for maybe the last 20 or 30 years of my life. What a thought." His sadness was seeping out of him. "It feels like a life sentence. I've never been alone. I've always had someone there for me."

"Ha! That reminds me of an old friend of mine who used to run a course, Preparing for Your Own Funeral, and when he died, it turned out that he'd made no plans whatsoever for his own funeral!"

But he was digressing and quickly returned to Clem's problem: "What about your girls? At least you've got them and you said you get on well with them."

"Yes, but they lead busy, complicated lives. Because Jasmine lives in Melbourne, I don't get to see her very much, and Jade, who's just broken up with her partner, is struggling as a single mother. I can't expect her to be babysitting me as well as her son. He's five. I wouldn't want her to do that anyway."

Zach shrugged and suggested he go and stay for a few weeks with Jasmine. Also, maybe help out with Jade's boy. Clem screwed up his face.

"Jasmine works full-time and often has to travel interstate in her job. I'd be on my own there most of the time or alone with her partner and I've never really taken to him. As for helping out with my grandson, I'm no good at that sort of thing. I left that to Greta."

"Well, now's the right time to step up," Zach replied, punching the air with a fist.

LOSS SURVIVOR

ZACH DIDN'T LEAVE any room for Clem to disagree. Instead, he swiftly changed the focus of the conversation and started talking about his parents. His mother died 18 years ago, three months before his father retired.

"Work distracted him from his grief and sense of loss but once he had nowhere to go during the day — bang — it all really hit him. Hard."

"That's where I'm at right now."

"Exactly, my friend! Exactly." Clem could feel Zach's enthusiasm. "I remember how he was ready to give up on life. Me and my sister did as much as we could for him." Counting off each item on his fingers, he went on: "We cooked meals, took him out, had him over, even tried to get him to play bowls and tried to find him something to do — anything, for goodness' sake! But we failed every time. We just couldn't get him to snap out of it."

"It's the worst feeling. It's not something you can snap out of just like that."

"Right. I know that now. At the time, we were guilty of looking for a quick fix. We didn't understand then."

"So, did he ever get through it?"

"Eventually. These things take time. The only thing that he did was potter around in his garden, pulling out weeds and trying not very hard to grow stuff. Gardening was never really his thing, you know. But he was so miserable. He was always complaining — it was always too hot or too cold outside. He complained about everything." Again, he counted on his fingers. "The news, his old firm, his new neighbours, his car, his health, us. My sister, in particular, increasingly lost it with him when he had a go at her or me."

"You didn't?"

"Nah. I've got a thick skin. It goes with my thick head! It takes a lot to push me over the edge, but I did come close a few times with Dad."

He qualified that by conceding that his "dear old sister" bore the brunt of their dad's moods. Zach was flat out with his job — he was a school principal, he explained — and didn't spend as much time with his dad as his sister did. Then, claiming that Clem "wouldn't believe the workload and the number of problems that my staff came to me with," he went off on a tangent. He told the story of an affair between two of the teachers and how it had a great impact on the rest of his staff.

Clem's attention drifted, firstly to a student, probably a uni student, at a nearby table working on her laptop. She looked Japanese and it made him think about the girl in Uniqlo. Then he returned to the kind of thoughts that Greta's death had unleashed. How every week seemed to bring him news of another death of some high-profile person who was a familiar figure in his youth. It was to be expected at this stage of his life. Celebrities he admired in his youth were now in their 80s or 90s. With each death, it was like another light being switched off and darkness was creeping all through the once brilliantly lit building — his life. It was so depressing. Soon there might well be virtually no one left from his 1960s teenage years or even his 1970s newly married years. From this miserable line of thought, it was a short step to the ominous question, "What's the point in living?"

As Zach continued telling the lurid and long-winded tale of his two teachers' affair, Clem shook himself free of his wandering thoughts, almost literally, with a faint shudder. He reprimanded himself for getting distracted. The story of Zach's father interested him but the teachers' affair didn't. Nor did he want to get obsessed about a young Japanese woman who flitted so momentarily through his life. Instead he wanted to know more about Zach's father. How did he get over his grief and loneliness? So he abruptly interrupted Zach's story about the teachers with a curt "What about your father?"

"Oh, my dad, yes." Zach felt bad about getting sidetracked. "Sorry. Thanks for getting me back from my walkabout."

So, getting back on track, he related the story of when his sister had coffee one day with a friend of hers and was complaining, as she often did, about her "old man".

"She probably included a moan or two about me not pulling my weight and leaving her to do the heavy lifting. And she was probably right. Anyway, this friend suddenly came up with the idea of getting her dad to meet our dad."

"Was he a widower too?"

"No, his wife was still very much alive and they were happily married. You see, Clem, even in this very different day and age you're not the only couple who have stayed happily married forever!"

The friend's dad was retired and involved in all sorts of activities and groups. Thoroughly enjoying retirement. Although Zach's sister didn't think anything would shift her dad's attitude, and doubted he would even agree to meet this total stranger, she was desperate enough to give it a try. She would try and coax him into having coffee with this other dad.

"Was it a battle for her?"

"You bet it was. It took her several goes before he reluctantly agreed to have coffee with him. Funny thing is, he never drinks coffee, so we knew he'd be hard to convince. Just as it would be hard to convince you."

Clem raised his eyebrows and smiled. Zach explained that all the grief, loneliness and sense of life being futile was "incredibly hard to shake". What he went through with his dad opened his eyes to that and Zach really felt for him, knew how hard it must have been for him to drag himself up out of the quagmire.

"Even my feisty, impatient sister — I love her really — got to understand that! Grief can completely smother you. It makes it hard to see any way out because you are in a sort of total darkness and the safety net has gone."

Clem had an impatient daughter too and he knew how Zach's father must have felt. Only the previous night, Jasmine lectured him at some length on the phone about how it was time to pull himself together and move on. As if he could just forget about Greta at the snap of his daughter's fingers! She had a busy life in Melbourne and she had problems of her own. Greta suspected that all was not well between Jasmine and her partner.

"She thinks that marriage is redundant these days but I don't think we would have survived if we hadn't been married. Not committing to marriage means they're also not committing to a lifelong relationship."

Not that she ever mentioned it to either of their unmarried girls. And he certainly wasn't interested in raising it with Jasmine now — what did he know anyway about relationships? Greta was the expert on that sort of thing, although he didn't like her comment about how they were lucky to have stayed together. She was probably thinking of that terrible time he was caught cheating on her and she forgave him. She probably thought they only survived that storm because they were formally welded together rather than just living together without the glue of marriage. But they never revisited that painful episode. They buried it, never to be dug up again.

The girls had a lot on their minds and he couldn't expect them to understand, but Zach was different. He'd only known him for a few minutes but he was warming to him. He asked him if the other dad clicked with Zach's father when they finally met for coffee.

"Hmm, Dad was — what's the word? — wary. For a start, the guy was South African — white South African — and Dad had had some bad experiences with a couple of South Africans. That created prejudice in him against all South Africans."

As he spoke, a man with black skin walked past muttering to himself and Zach lowered his voice.

"At least his beef was with the white ones, not the black ones."

Raising his voice again, he continued: "He also convinced himself that the friend's dad only went because his daughter had ordered him to do it. Admittedly, my sister's friend is pretty bossy — according to my sister — but, hey, it takes one to know one, as they say. Still, you can always find negatives if you want, can't you?"

Clem smiled. Zach sounded like Greta. She was always the positive force in their marriage and Clem usually the doubting Thomas.

"Don't think of cancer as a death sentence. I'm going to get through it, you see. I intend on being at my grandson's wedding and I expect you to be there with me as well."

"The friend's dad was— as my father would say — 'a gasbag'. He did most of the talking. OK, OK. That's me too, you're thinking, I know! But hey, you don't have to point that out to me! Despite all my dad's doubts though, this guy critically invited him over for dinner a few weeks later."

To Clem's surprise, Zach's father agreed to go, although he needed a lot of persuading. His sister gave Zach that job because he was "better at the sweet-talking stuff". His father made it clear, however, that his well-intentioned but naïve children were trying to find a simple solution to a complicated problem. And it wouldn't work.

"I remember him saying, 'I know you and your sister are trying to fix me and you think all will be well if I just go out and meet people, but I can't replace your mother just by having chats with a stranger.' Much later, not long before he died actually, he reminded me of that remark and how wrong he'd been and how grateful he was to us for pushing him."

Dead? That was a real disappointment. Clem had assumed Zach's father was still alive and he had been starting to think that he'd like to meet him. To even be thinking like that was a surprisingly positive change of attitude. Putting that setback aside, Clem asked what happened when Zach's father went to the dinner date.

"This was the big breakthrough. The friend's dad — his name was Walter — had invited a couple of other friends. One was a bloke who was divorced and the other was a widow. It was nice that he invited single people, not another couple, don't you think?"

Walter's wife was there too and Zach's dad "took a shine" to her. She was a great cook and it was the dinner she prepared that won him over.

Clem laughed. "The way to a man's heart is through his stomach. Greta was a good cook, so I know what I'm talking about!"

"Exactly. But all four of them played a part in winning Dad over. Three of them belonged to the same religious faith and the fourth one, the divorced guy, was another lonely soul like my dad."

"Did they try to get your dad involved in their church? It would certainly put me off because I have no interest in religion and can see a religious hijack coming a mile off."

"Good job they didn't invite you along then," Zach joked. "No, as far as I know, they didn't push their religion on Dad or even talk about it, other than explaining that link between them. They were just doing what all religious people should do. They were extending the hand of friendship."

Zach added that he wasn't religious either and would have warned off his dad if he was walking into a recruitment drive. Then he described the two single people at the dinner. The man's wife had gone off with someone else after about 25 years of marriage and he was alone.

"He hadn't seen it coming. Us blokes often don't see what's obvious. Maybe he hadn't been a great husband or father. I really don't know. But he was another one that Walter and his wife had taken under their wing."

The woman was widowed longer than Zach's dad, about five years.

That dinner was apparently the turning point. After that, the five of them started seeing each other regularly over dinner or morning catch-ups at cafés. Zach's dad and the other single man, Riadh, even joined a bowling club. The name, Riadh, surprised Clem. He had mentally imagined him as a white Australian but Riadh was a Middle Eastern name. He may even have been a Muslim. Not a Todd or a Bruce. In fact, Zach reckoned three of the group — Walter and his wife and Riadh — came to Australia as migrants or refugees.

Zach said that Riadh had lived in a few different countries but was originally from Iraq and had been in Australia for about 10 years at the time. The widow was born and bred in Perth. She was the only "full Aussie" at the dinner table. Again, this revelation took Clem by surprise because he had assumed, wrongly, that Zach's father was Australian born. It turned out he was a Hungarian who came to Australia as a refugee child after the Second World War.

"But you would never have known if you'd met him. He had no Hungarian accent and was mad about the cricket. He loved Warnie. How Australian is that?!"

Returning to the outcome of the dinner, Zach said the five of them all got on really well together. He attributed a lot of that to Walter. He was the driving force and had a really good way of making people comfortable.

Like Zach himself, thought Clem. He glanced at his watch. They'd been chatting for no more than 20 or 30 minutes and Zach already sounded like a long-time friend. He hadn't chatted like this with anyone for ages. Especially not a complete stranger and certainly not since his wife's passing. Zach noticed him sneaking a look at his watch and apologised for taking up so much of his time. Clem laughed. As if he had anywhere else to go or anything else to do!

"Time is something I've got far too much of these days but don't let me keep you if you need to get on," Clem said.

END IN SIGHT

ACTUALLY, ZACH DID have to be somewhere shortly. He explained he was due at the hospital — now it was his turn to look at his watch — in a few minutes. He stood and put his Akubra back on, ready to go.

"Hospital? Why have you got to go there?"

"It's my son. He came off his motorbike last night and he's in surgery."

"Is it life-threatening?"

"God, no. He broke his leg and a few other bones. It should be enough of a wake-up call for him to ditch bikes for good but it'll probably just keep him off the road for a couple of months." The look on Clem's face betrayed his shock at this news. "Riding those things is a death wish. My son should know that by now but he still thinks like a teenager. Thinks he's bulletproof."

Maybe not life-threatening but it was still mighty serious, yet Zach had sat talking as if this was just another uneventful day. How could he be so detached from what was happening to his son? Clem looked away to a nearby table where two teenage boys were studying together. Two boys yet to discover the thrills and dangerous spills of motorbikes.

"You're shocked, right? Shocked that I'm talking to you about your problems and telling you about my dad's own crisis rather than telling you all about my son."

"That's right. You seem so relaxed. So untroubled."

It was his way of coping, Zach explained. When he was stressed, he absorbed himself in other people's lives. Often it put his own problems into perspective, he said. Zach looked down and started picking at his fingernails. Then, looking up again, he continued. He wasn't sure that he should use others like Clem as a means of finding a way through his own "darkness", he said. "It definitely went very dark when I got the call about the accident last night."

"You really shouldn't think like that. I don't feel used. Quite the opposite in fact. You've perked me up." Then, turning to his own "darkness", he asked: "Could I let you in on a little secret? Have you got just five minutes more?"

Yes, he absolutely wanted to hear about the secret but only if Clem was sure about sharing it with him and — forgetting his own need to get to the hospital — if Clem had enough time to spare. He sat down again.

Clem began tentatively. "I've been so down since I lost Greta that I have thought about, you know, ending it all. Suicide." He uttered the word, suicide, with audible embarrassment. "I've not talked to anyone about this." Zach sat back down heavily. "At first, I thought I couldn't do that to my daughters but then I got to think-ing that I'm no use to them anyway. They'd cope OK without me."

Zach stared at him. "Losing you would devastate them."

"I don't think so. I've never really helped them much with their problems. I left all that to Greta."

Zach said it was all the more reason for them to need their dad and added that his daughter would have given anything for a dad like Clem. But Clem didn't see himself in such a kindly light. Grief was blinding him. He remembered being so destroyed by the prospect of Greta dying that he told her he would rather kill himself than carry on without her.

"Don't you dare even think of doing that. That would be weak and selfish and you're neither of those things. You're strong. Pull yourself together!"

He'd promised her that he would be strong but it was proving hard to keep his promise. He wasn't as strong as she thought he was. Every day now he felt like giving up.

Zach was still trying to take in what Clem had just told him. "Look, I'm no counsellor but I've had to deal with suicides. You must never ever think like that," Zach said as if channelling Greta. "Promise me, my friend!" He paused for a response but Clem didn't give one. Zach felt the need to be more forceful with him. "I'll show you why suicide is a terrible idea. Let me share a little secret of my own. It might make you realise that you can get through this."

"This really is secret men's business then."

Zach took off his hat and placed it on the floor. He leaned forward, elbows resting on his knees, and stared at his shoes. He spoke so quietly that it was hard for Clem to hear him, so he asked if Zach could start again and speak louder. When he resumed, still looking down — Clem could hear him better, though not well — Zach took him back to the year 1982 and the death of his first wife, Ellie.

He and Ellie were married for 11 years and had two children, a boy and a girl. The marriage was fine at first but then everything went down "a very steep hill" after the birth of their second child, Philippa. He said she was known to everyone except him as Pip. He always used her full first name. Although he knew it was "unAustralian", he'd never been one for shortening names. Clem frowned. Wasn't Ellie short for Eleanor? But now wasn't the time to nitpick so he let it go.

Zach said his wife would attack him for no real reason. She accused him of having an affair with a friend's wife. That was totally untrue. Accused him of not being interested in the kids. Again untrue. Almost every day they would argue. Ellie more than held her own in the frequent fights but she was becoming more and more erratic. Her neighbour and good friend, Rasmina, sometimes looked after Ellie's kids for an hour or so but she stopped doing that after

Ellie disappeared for over three hours one day while Rasmina had the kids. She had to get her husband to take time off work to collect their own two children from school. He was furious and demanded that she not have Ellie's kids again. Then, when she refused to let Ellie leave her kids with her, Ellie swore at her, only to be angelically sweet the next time she saw her. Some days Ellie would be this lovely friend, concerned that Rasmina and her husband, Egyptian migrants, were struggling financially, and then another day Ellie might walk past her without saying a word or staring at her like a tormented soul. For Rasmina, it was like dealing with two different people. And Ellie was like this with others, too.

Zach worried about the effect on their children of all his arguments with Ellie. Dylan was just four and Pip had only just had her first birthday. And what was their mother's wild behaviour and mood swings doing to them? One evening Zach and Ellie had yet another furious argument. The kids were awake and heard it all, he said, running a hand through his thin head of grey hair as if that would brush away some of his shame. And in the heat of the row, he told her that he was going to divorce her.

"The next day was the worst day of my life."

The day after the big argument, Zach came home to a silent and empty house. He assumed she was out somewhere with the children but it was almost 5.30. The children should be at home and she should be feeding them. Then he thought perhaps she had pre-empted his divorce threat and left him, taking the children with her. So he checked the bedrooms. No evidence of flight there.

Coming back downstairs, he turned on the kettle and reached down for a mug out of the cupboard under the kitchen bench. And it was then that he saw the unimaginable. Looking up from the floor, Zach told Clem that it was many times more shocking than the most frightening of scenes in a movie. She had hanged herself from a wooden beam on their patio. With his heart beating wildly, he rushed outside to try and save her. He got her down onto the ground but it was too late. She was dead.

"Rasmina heard my wailing and climbed over the fence — something I couldn't have imagined her ever doing. She threw her arms around me and we wailed together. It was definitely not like her, a devout, dignified Muslim, to throw herself at a man like that."

Clem quietly gasped. He wasn't usually a touchy-feely kind of person but put a consoling hand on Zach's shoulder. "How terrible. For you and your children."

Both men sat silently with their thoughts. Clem had plenty of arguments over the years with Greta but they always repaired the damage fairly quickly, often through compromise. Even after his brief affair there was never any serious talk of divorce. But he had to do a lot of apologising and Greta had to do a lot of forgiving. Yet, since Greta's death, he was filled with remorse about how often he failed her. The times he wasn't very understanding or sympathetic and too caught up in work dramas; the times he did what he wanted to do rather than what she wanted.

Now death was unleashing an unbearable pain because it was too late to give Greta his remorse, and he was desperate to do just that. Yet his pain was nothing compared with what Zach must have gone through, which was probably why he was telling him all this. Then Clem thought about what it would be like for his daughters if he gave up and did the same as Ellie. Greta would be furious.

"How could you do that to our children? The guilt you've dumped on them! They'll be tormented with thinking they should have done more, that it's their fault. Like hell, it is! They've done nothing wrong. This is all down to you. How pathetic!"

Zach, now looking directly at Clem, broke the silence, saying it was awful that Ellie took her own life and awful for him to find her. But then he had to face the ordeal of everyone else's reactions. They blamed him, especially his children and Ellie's family. That was so unfair, he said forcefully.

But he got through it all, just as he told Clem he would get through his grief. And just as his dad got through losing his wife. The situations were different but there was always a key figure who came to the rescue. For him, it was his mother. She was instrumental in getting him, eventually, to move on and start not just a new chapter but a new book.

That new book involved falling in love with another woman, he said with a broad smile.

"We've been married almost 25 years and, you know what — I still haven't found any faults in her! Every day I have to pinch myself that she is real, that my life is real and that I am happier than I have ever been."

He slapped Clem on the thigh, the sort of intimacy from which Clem would normally recoil, but he didn't flinch.

"The point is it's always darkest before the dawn. It's a cliché but it's true. You might be in despair but there's always a light out there waiting for you to find it. Sometimes the light even finds you. Never give up, hard as life is."

Clem wasn't convinced but didn't want to say so. He felt Zach deserved a more positive response.

"Well, let's hope you're right," he said. "You've certainly given me some food for thought. I doubt I could have offered you as much help when you lost your wife."

Zach laid a hand firmly on Clem's shoulder and laughed. He was adamant that Clem would have been there for him if they'd known each other then and he insisted that he'd gained the most out of "this little chat". Clem didn't agree but suggested that they compromise and settle for a draw — each of them getting as much as the other out of the conversation.

"All right," conceded Zach, "but declaring a draw does go against my male competitive spirit, you know. No one wins when it's a draw!"

Clem, concerned that he was keeping Zach from his son, suggested he should go to the hospital. Zach seemed relaxed about it and Clem, taking this as encouragement to detain him, asked how old his son was.

"Old enough to know better. Dylan's 44. We're not as close as we should be. He's never completely forgiven me for his mother's death. We didn't get on at all for a long time. When I met and married Genevieve, our relationship improved. I owe so much to her. But that's a story for another time, as is the story of my daughter. Right now, though, I really should go."

Both men stood and Zach ignored a proffered handshake to give Clem a prolonged bear hug. Clem wasn't a hugger, even with his daughters and even, ashamedly, with his wife. The hug trapped his arms. He felt silly. Suddenly, this whole conversation with Zach seemed silly. This wasn't who Clem was. At 72, did he really want to become a different person, hugging other men and putting his life in another man's hands? He'd always coped with setbacks by being himself. Toughing it out.

"Don't be so silly. Don't be frightened of your emotions and expressing them."

Yes, Greta, he thought, he had let his emotions loose with Zach, talking about what he was going through. Everyone else seemed embarrassed by his grief and preferred safer topics of conversation, often talking about themselves and what they were doing. And he could understand that. Letting your emotions out of the bottle was very uncomfortable but it didn't make Zach uncomfortable. Quite the reverse — it precipitated the story of his wife's suicide. Yet ... this bear hug reminded Clem that he was on dangerous ground.

The hug seemed to last longer than it did. Clem was conscious of others in the library looking at them. Then, finally, Zach released him and Clem wondered how they would end this encounter. Would he ever see Zach again? All things considered, it would be a shame if this were a one-off, never to be repeated. But despite the doubts now rising in him, he would welcome talking again with him. Then as if Zach once again knew what Clem was thinking, he was the first to speak, insisting that they exchange contact details.

"I've got someone I'd like you to meet," he said.

Clem hesitated to ask who but he went ahead and asked anyway with surprising emotional boldness.

"Is it Walter?"

"Got it in one."

COMING HOME

THAT EVENING CLEM'S phone pinged when a new text message landed. His daughter, Jasmine, wanted to have a FaceTime chat. He suggested doing it the next day as that would be Saturday. He anticipated that it would be easier for her to make time for him at the weekend.

"No NOW!" she wrote back and added a string of emojis.

Clem sighed. It was 9.30 and he wasn't in the mood for another lecture from her like yesterday's. But then he realised that it was 11.30 for her. She should be in bed. Oh no, he thought, this would be bad news because she never rang that late at night. Even in the days immediately before and after Greta's death, she almost always stuck to daytime calls. But as he mulled over his response options, Jasmine decided for him by calling him anyway on FaceTime. His iPad seemed unable to contain her beaming face. Her long blonde hair, with those risky blue and purple streaks, bounced on her shoulders as she playfully shook her head from side to side.

"Look, Jazzy, I'm more than happy to chat but please go easy," he said before either of them had said hello or asked how they were. "No more lectures. Please."

"And good evening to you, too, Dad," she laughed before going through a pretend exchange with him. "How's your day been? Oh good, I'm glad to hear that you went out. Did you see the news tonight? No, it's all too depressing … " Then she noticed the shirt that Clem was wearing. "Oh my god, is that shirt new? I've never seen you in anything quite so … so sexy!"

He smiled and explained that he'd bought it that day at Uniqlo. "It's not really me, is it? Red and yellow, I mean."

"It's f-a-n-t-a-s-t-i-c, Dad. Be careful though. You'll have women chasing after you."

"Haha, very funny. Why this late-night call? You're normally asleep at this time."

Jasmine threw back her head and wiped a hand across her forehead like a tennis player who's just crucially lost her serve. While still doing that, she uttered a ponderous "Well". Her change of mood did not bode well. Clem adopted the brace position, as he often did with her.

Resuming a more relaxed pose but now with a grave expression, Jasmine began: "Well, you were right to tell me 'no more lectures'. I want to apologise. I was out of order yesterday when I laid down the law and told you to get on with things and put all this about Mum behind you. I'm so sorry, Dad."

"You weren't brutal," Clem responded without being entirely truthful.

"Yes, I was and I need to walk in your shoes a whole lot more."

"You'll struggle because my shoes are much too big for you."

"It'll be karma for me then. Look, I made a big decision today that I haven't been there for you and it's high time that I was."

She paused and Clem, already floored by her apology, didn't know what to make of this. Was it all just words or was she actually going to turn words into some kind of action?

"Look, I didn't get much sleep last night. I realised that I've … "

She scrunched up her eyes and bowed her head, her hair falling over her eyes. Clem told her not to upset herself but beyond that, he was lost because he didn't know what it was that she had "realised". There was a long pause and when she finally raised her head, she was crying.

"I realised that I've been a lousy daughter, a lousy sister and a lousy aunt," she blurted as she tried and failed to suppress emotion.

"No, no, Jazzy, you haven't. Not at all."

"So I decided today that I'm going to take leave from my job and come over."

"Oh, that'll be lovely but you really don't have to drop everything for me. I'm coping OK."

"And while I'm there I'm going to look for a job in Perth."

"Ivan too?"

"Of course." Her voice cracked. "He's on board with it."

"Are you sure about that? He's lived all his life in Melbourne."

Jasmine insisted that her partner was definitely happy to come to Perth. Clem, ever the cynic, wasn't convinced but now wasn't the time to make an issue of it. Instead he repeated, with more emphasis, that it would be fantastic, rather than just lovely, to see her and, of course, she could stay with him.

"So when are you planning on coming?"

"Tomorrow."

SLEEPING PARTNER

A FEW MINUTES later, as he lay in bed propped up against two pillows with his book open in front of him but not reading it, he tried to digest the events of the day. His life had been barren for weeks. He had been dining on nothing but grief. It was grim fare. Today, by comparison, was a feast, although he was having some trouble trying to digest it all. It remained to be seen where it would lead, but at least he now had cause for hope.

He looked at the empty space beside him in the bed. As happened every night when he did this, he felt every seam of his heart straining to bursting point. It still hurt not to have Greta there with him. And, as always, he could see her and he began to talk to her.

"Sweetheart, it's been a better day today. The best one since … you know what. What do you think of Zach? I enjoyed talking with him and hearing about how his father coped after his wife's death. Poor guy. Imagine coming home and finding that your wife has killed herself."

"No, I can't imagine that at all."

"I think it wasn't just me dumping on him. He's got issues of his own.

"Hasn't everyone?"

"Maybe I can help him as much as he can help me. That'd be funny — me as a counsellor. Who'd have thought it!"

"You've always been blind to your qualities and told yourself you're not good enough, not skilled enough. I'm glad you're starting to think differently."

"But I'm not used to opening up like I did today. It's not fair burdening others with my pain."

"Why is it that men have such difficulty talking about emotional things, eh? You've got nothing to lose."

"I've already lost too much."

"Away with you, Clem! You've got plenty still to live for."

"Then there's Jasmine hotfooting it over here all of a sudden and talking about abandoning Melbourne. So unlike her."

"That's a bit harsh, Clem."

"I hope Ivan really is OK about the idea of moving to Perth. I'm not so sure."

"Nor am I."

"But I've got to admit, I've never known Jazzy to be as open-hearted as she was tonight. She's always kept her distance from me."

"That's not true."

"And I've never really taken to Ivan."

"It will be a chance to get to know him better if he's going to live over here. Who knows, maybe they'll decide to get married. Wouldn't that be good?"

He picked up his book, not many pages left, but, as he continued to process his day, weariness took over. The book slid from his hands and he fell asleep.

ESSAYS

A WALK IN THE PARK

I took a walk in the woods and came out
taller than the trees.

— Henry David Thoreau

I SIT ON a log in the city park at the side of an extravagant pathway of grass. It stretches in a straight line to my left for more than a kilometre. Urban bushland borders each side. A city tower looms a safe distance away behind the trees facing me on the other side of this green carpet. Disappearing into the distance is a woman and her white dog, as well as a jogger dressed in black. I watch them turning into specks on the end of my index finger. And then I think about another park that has receded into a speck on the rim of my memory.

It was Hyde Park in London almost 50 years ago. I'd started my first job after leaving school five months earlier and it was a Friday evening in November at the end of the working week. I had an hour to fill before meeting a friend and going together to a concert at the Royal Albert Hall across the road from the almost deserted park. And alone in the dark and damp of my early evening solitude, I journeyed into the virgin forest of my soul. I couldn't see the beauty of the park itself but I wandered into a kind of spell with nothing to catch my eye or ear — the distant hum of evening traffic was dead to me. Unfettered and relishing the music that awaited me at the concert in the fabled old concert hall, I roamed far from the well-trodden path of daily routine. I was in a place I hadn't visited before. It didn't look like anything I knew but the evening breeze had followed me down this pathway and was dancing through the trees. I was in a new landscape, me and it hiding in the darkness.

Kings Park, Perth. It is a warm spring day. The sky is cloudless and fiercely bright, a world away from that London darkness. Again, I am journeying alone. I am looking back 50 years, watching that far-off speck of discovery. The memory and this day invite me to return to that soulful forest, a place I should visit more often. I have abandoned the depths of the real me for the trip wires of daily routine and aggrandisement. I need to veer off-track and lose myself in the forest. Really lose myself, and not just for a few minutes; in a wild place, not a manicured city park. This park now and that park then are just glimpses into another world. Advertisements with no seductive voiceovers or special offers. No bookings necessary. Just go. Then go farther.

> *I will arise and go now, for always night and day*
> *I hear lake water lapping with low sounds by the shore;*
> *While I stand on the roadway, or on the pavements grey,*
> *I hear it in the deep heart's core.*
>
> (W.B. Yeats, The Lake Isle of Innisfree)

• **In memory of Joe, who went to that concert and whose London was a magical place.**

IT'S THE SIXTIES ALL OVER AGAIN

You got me singing
Like a prisoner in a jail
You got me singing
Like my pardon's in the mail
— Leonard Cohen, You Got Me Singing

SO, THEY DIDN'T organise one of those surprise birthday parties. You know how it goes. Just when you think you'll safely survive the day, your wife or daughter (it's always a female) suggests visiting someone. Unsuspecting, you go along with her. As you enter the house, your wife/daughter strangely dropping back behind you, all is as it should be. Or so you misguidedly think. You turn a corner and, suddenly, 5000 friends are waiting for you with big grins on their faces and yelling: "S-U-R-P-R-I-S-E!"

You smile benignly at everyone. Actually, you're quite humbled that so many people have turned out for you, even though you hate being the centre of so much attention, but there are one or two unfamiliar faces ... Then as cynicism returns to its natural habitat, you start to wonder if they've all been paid to be here.

Well, the other week was my 60th and I struck early: I made it plain that I didn't want any surprise parties. But that didn't necessarily mean the family would pay heed to my demand. My smart bomb wouldn't necessarily find its target and wipe out the suspected weapons of mass surprise. I needn't have worried. There were no such weapons. And perhaps that was for the best at my advanced age.

Funny things, big birthdays. They make you slightly paranoid – as in slightly pregnant. A 60-something friend told me recently that he hadn't been bothered so much about turning 30, 40 or 50, but 60 really hurt. He finally got the message that he was old. Now it's my turn and it did cross my mind in the last week of my fifties when I stumbled — by accident of course — on singer Shakira gyrating provocatively on TV that, after December 26, showing a normal manly interest in such goings-on would qualify me as a dirty old man.

I have noticed that when you reach a "certain age", sometime in your middle to late fifties, your contemporaries start asking in shocked tones: "You're still working?" Retirement has gone to the top of their conversation agenda, along with superannuation, health issues and nostalgia. Increasingly, sentences start, "When I was that age, we would never ... " and we talk a lot about life before computers.

People also start to give up their seats for you on trains and buses. It happened to me for the first time last year on a train in England from Gatwick Airport to Eastbourne. Didn't the fat geezer know that I was in far better shape than him (I swim, for God's sake!) and he really needed the seat more than I did? Still, at least in Eastbourne, aka God's Waiting Room because so many people there are retirees, I felt young again. Everyone else was so much older than me, even in the wannabe-hip Caffe Nero, dubbed Caffe Zero by my son. That's hip as in cool, not as in hip replacement.

The adverts insist that the best you can hope for beyond the age of 60 is to sit around all day in the sun drinking wine with your "friends" in the retirement village (the ones you always moan about afterwards), playing endless rounds of golf or bowls or cards, joining thousands of other oldies on "luxury" cruises and never again having to get up early … unless your bladder's bursting, which it usually is because, let's face it, you're OLD.

I don't want to live in a "village" where everyone's a retiree and most are over about 70; I don't drink wine; and golf, bowls and cruises are of no interest to me. I want more than fool's gold from my "golden years".

Trouble is, I've reached an age where I can plan all I like for my future but I may not get there. My father died at the age of 62. I am very conscious of that. Was it really 30 years ago? His retirement was over before it had barely started. Ouch, that hurts. And there's still so much I want to do. You know, to make a mark. To elevate my life out of the ordinary.

So what do I want? I was a child of the Sixties and now I am a man of the sixties, but it's taken a long time to reach adulthood — almost 50 years, because I was 12 when the Beatles had their first number one, heralding the real start of the decade that shaped my life, and I turned 60 two weeks after Leonard Cohen gave possibly his last-ever concert.

Leonard Cohen, you ask? Yes, because the Beatles stood for all that was vibrant and swinging about the Sixties and Cohen is my marker for the start of a hopefully vibrant New Sixties. I have bestowed this honour on him because during his comeback tour at the age of 74 Cohen talked about when he last toured — at the age of 60. "I was just a kid with a crazy dream," he deadpanned.

I like this idea of being a kid with a crazy dream. OK, I know Lenny's "dream" appears to have involved bunkering down and doing some serious soul-searching in a Buddhist monastery up a mountain for 10 years while he was robbed blind by his manager. That might not appeal to everyone as a way of spending your sixties, but I like it. He stopped and took stock — although not, sadly, of what his manager was doing. It's a good time to press pause.

I'm already up a mountain ... in my mind. I'm doing some soul-searching too. I'm trying to puzzle things out because, in many ways, the world and I went separate ways this past decade and I have become a bit of a monk — minus the haircut and the robes but definitely cloistered, albeit prosaically around my computer.

My problem is that whereas once I was filled with drive and optimism, even when the going got tough, I have become lethargic and dogged by disappointment. All that effort to make the world a better place and it just seems to be getting worse. Doesn't God know I have a deadline to meet?

Working in the old media (newspapers), I spend my days at the epicentre of the storm: forced to edit endless so-called stories about materialism, "lifestyle" (think cruises and chefs), vacuous celebrities and opportunistic politicians whose beliefs swing with the latest polls. News and analysis are stuffed into the endlessly hungry jaws of the internet and social media. These ever-faster forms of technology come with an addiction to style and "product" over substance, not to mention a love of bigotry masquerading as informed opinion.

At the same time, we have collectively walked out on the idea of spiritual pursuit — sacrificed to consumerism, science and general disillusionment with religion. Yet consumerism is only a short-lived fix, scientific "proof" is transitory and religion is not the same thing as God. Where does God say that priests have to be celibate? For 40 years I have followed a faith that makes much more sense to me than anything on offer from other religions or political parties. It has the answers to everything and yet hardly anyone — relative, friend or colleague — sees what I see. So I'm beginning to understand why Cohen went up the mountain and stayed there a long time. I'm frustrated that even when people know things have to change, they won't let go of their caution and distractions.

As Cohen put it in his song, The Future: " … *the blizzard of the world / Has crossed the threshold and it's overturned / The order of the soul.*"

And so here I am up a mountain, mentally speaking, regrouping (can an individual in solitary confinement re*group*?) and trying to get pumped up again for action because I don't want to spend the rest of my life driven by frustration into doing nothing and feeling angry at the world. You know, like those Grumpy Old Men on television. Luckily, I've not chosen to go up a creek without a paddle but it's mighty lonely on the mountainside as I try to absorb the lesson that difficulties can be a source of strength; that darkness is only the absence of light.

Or as Cohen, more hopefully, again explains in Anthem: *"There is a crack in everything / That's how the light gets in."*

My hope is that when you step back from the daily rush — yes, go up a mountain if you like — it will be possible to see the cracks more clearly and, therefore, the light that shines no matter how bad things get. Many years ago I went up into the mountains around Lake Geneva. It was my first serious mountain and I saw into the cracks that day. Going up a mountain is like when you're in a plane climbing through the clouds out of the grey and wet into the sunshine, which was always there only you couldn't see it.

So I need to do some mountaineering as I venture forth into the New Sixties. It's called getting my act together and getting a clearer sighting of the "crazy dream".

John Lennon was another dreamer who offers hope in his song, *Imagine*: *"You may say I'm a dreamer / But I'm not the only one / I hope someday you'll join us / And the world will be as one."*

A world as one was my original dream, and still is. It's not that crazy, is it? No, it just needs some new energy and there's no reason why 60-year-olds can't be as energetic as anyone. Leonard Cohen still skips on and off stage; gets down on one knee and gets up again unaided. Hopefully, there's some accumulated wisdom and experience that will help me as well.

But I'm not after the kind of energy that it takes to run at the pace of modern life. The merry-go-round has definitely sped up and from my mountain perch it looks like everyone's running faster and faster, trying to keep up and hopefully leap on the spinning contraption that they're chasing. But they're just running around in circles and they'll never be able to make that leap or to keep on running (cue the Spencer Davis Group's 1960s hit Keep on Running). They'll run out of energy and scream: "Somebody help me" (cue second Spencer Davis 1960s hit Somebody Help Me).

Opting out of the fast lane, however, doesn't mean I'm ready for the retirement village and the bowling green. I'm just trying to find some of my accumulated wisdom (don't laugh) and apply it.

I want the ability to think clearly and to ward off whatever assaults the world can throw at me. Maybe I should quit my job, distance myself from media madness and loosen the chains that bind me to big mortgages. Maybe I need to find my inner hippie. Maybe the answer is to write books, even if they sell by the tens rather than the thousands. Maybe I need to do something I haven't even thought of yet.

There's certainly a job for me to do as a parent and a grandparent because children and grandchildren need role models and mentors. After all, they have to deal with the merry-go-round as well. I'm thinking that they need to know more about who their father/grandfather really is. I've kept myself too much to myself in the past. It's what Englishmen do, to everyone's detriment. The other day my daughter reprimanded me for never getting back to her when she asked me what kind of struggles my wife and I had when we were first married. In future, I need to answer questions like that, even if the agonising over taking out a £10,000 mortgage in Britain in the Seventies doesn't really stack up as a "struggle" in our contemporary Australian world of $500,000+ mortgages.

But this is not just about me. There's the whole challenge facing US of moving into OUR "twilight" years. I'm talking about me and Mrs Mountain. We're both 60-something teenagers, both determined not to end up in a retirement village or some care home of our son's choosing. We're both determined not to act our age. She's become a gym junkie; every morning I swim unimagined distances in shark-infested waters. She talks on her mobile — hands-free, officer — as she drives in heavy traffic; I start thinking straight when I stay up till one in the morning. She single-handedly keeps the Qantas and Virgin airlines solvent going to meetings in Sydney; I keep the planet's last record shop in business. We both wake up each morning before the alarm goes off but, tellingly, we yawn every five minutes.

How will we fare when our bodies start objecting to all this abuse? When we finally swallow our pride and apply for a seniors card? When we no longer work? When we have to spend the livelong day with each other — me who puts things away and she who leaves things out? When we start to forget each other's name? When our children plead with us to give up driving? When we start earning the cemetery board equivalent of frequent-flyer points because of all the funerals we're attending?

These are all challenges of growing old together. Not that we're old, of course. Denial, denial.

There's plenty for me to think about as I pass my days up here on the mountain. I don't want to be an old Grumpy — even though I've been doing a pretty passable imitation recently. For that to happen I must plug into the energy that feeds my dreams. It's not easy finding a free socket. Have you noticed how many more things we have to plug in these days and how there's never a socket without a plug in it? Wasn't like that when I was young. Harumph! Guess I've got to realign my thinking; work out how to make the New Sixties better than the Old Sixties.

Maybe it will work like this suggestion from Cohen's Anthem: *"Every heart, every heart / to love will come / but like a refugee."*

A MATTER OF LIFE AND DEATH

> *... mothers are the first educators, the first*
> *mentors; and truly it is the mothers who*
> *determine the happiness, the future greatness,*
> *the courteous ways and learning and*
> *judgment, the understanding and the faith of*
> *their little ones.*
>
> — 'Abdu'l-Bahá

THIS DAY 100 years ago my mother was born. No birthday cards, presents or message from the Queen are necessary because she died almost nine years ago. She's buried on the other side of the world with my father, so no flower-infused visits to the cemetery either. In fact, I am certain that no one will mark her centenary today by visiting her grave.

August 24, 1921. The "Great" War (nothing "great" about it) had ended three years earlier and decimated Britain's male population. The Spanish flu added even more decimation to the nation's suffering. Victory, what victory? But my grandparents, in London's

East End, survived it all and on this day had their only child. As if they hadn't suffered enough, however, the "Great" Depression wasn't far off (why were awful things "great" in those days?). Even worse, before my mother was out of her teens, another devastating world war started.

This time my mother was in the thick of it as a civilian bombed night after night by German planes in the London Blitz and later by "doodlebug" flying bombs. East Enders, bunkered down in air-raid shelters, would hear the doodlebugs arriving overhead and when the distinct noise of their flight cut out, they knew that they or their homes might be smashed into tiny pieces any second.

My mother, and her parents, survived but weeks and weeks of all this shredded her nerves and no doubt thousands of other people's. There was no internet or TV distraction available then. No counselling either. Just Vera Lynn and Glenn Miller but they weren't enough to clear the wreckage in people's heads. Everyone just had to keep their chins up and carry on. A Covid lockdown is nowhere near as tough.

Then, shortly after the war, my mother married her penfriend and I was born in 1950. For all but the first few weeks of my life we lived in Croydon, a 20-minute train ride from central London. Despite my parents' wartime experiences — my father fought at El-Alamein but never spoke about it — everything in our house was calm. My mother worried much more than she needed to but not to a stifling extent. Occasional arguments between my parents never escalated out of control. As far as I was concerned, my parents' marriage was rock solid.

I did nothing to embarrass them and excelled at school. At 18 I changed my mind about wanting to go to university and instead started a journalism cadetship on the local paper. At 19 I flew the nest for the first time to live nearby in a grubby house with some friends. My mother wasn't impressed with the dirt and mess in my new home. She grumbled but didn't rant and anyway, I soon returned home, unimpressed with some of the people in the house share. My mother had basically been right.

A year later I moved out again, this time sharing a big house in a swankier part of town with a work colleague and some other friends. My mother had always done all the cooking in our home. I barely ever made even a cup of tea or coffee. Now I found myself on a cooking roster and somehow managed to pull together some semi-passable offerings. I no longer depended on my parents and my mother in particular.

Increasingly, I saw less and less of her. After finishing my cadetship, I moved to a Kent newspaper, became a Bahá'í and got married. By then I had established a whole new network of friends, many of whom my parents had never met. We invited well over 100 people to our wedding and my mother found this swarm of unfamiliar faces quite overwhelming. She was a quiet, retiring type of person not used to being in a crowd.

Another test for her was the fact that my new in-laws were "from the North". My mother had rarely strayed from London and the Home Counties. Holidays were always in Hastings or the Isle of Wight and "the North" was a foreign country for her. It was a struggle but maybe the bigger struggle was coming to terms with the realisation that her only child now had a different dominant female figure in his life. She had lost that role and, now in her fifties and with no career, she was struggling to find a purpose for her remaining years. As with the war, she survived.

She still had my father, of course, but he was now in a senior management position on the local newspaper and under stress of his own. But he recognised that he had to do something to help my mother. He made sacrifices. He gave up his weekends, which most notably involved going to the football, to take her to Eastbourne on the Sussex coast where the fresh air calmed my mother's nerves.

Our first three children came in quick succession and my father's health wasn't too good so he took early retirement. They had grown to love Eastbourne and when he retired, they moved there. Then came two hammer blows for my mother.

My wife and I had been looking to move overseas, to somewhere warmer and drier. A place where nappies didn't have to be dried almost every day inside the house over a fire. I applied for jobs in Hong Kong, Bermuda and Cyprus but all to no avail. Almost as a last resort, we turned to Australia.

We were interviewed, had medicals and gathered that official approval would be a formality, albeit at the usual speed with which bureaucracy moved. We talked with my parents about this dramatic turn of events. We wanted them to consider moving to Australia too.

My mother had never been on a plane and had never been overseas. For her, Australia was akin to the Moon. She didn't say yes, didn't say no. So English. Instead, she deferred to my father. She would go along with whatever he decided. But, like her, he didn't come down on either side of the fence, indicating only that he had seen "enough" of the world during the war but he might be open to coming by ship. Reading between the lines, we didn't anticipate that they would follow us to the other side of the world.

While we were exploring the possibility of Australia and then waiting for the green light to go, my father's health got much worse. He was diagnosed with emphysema and overnight he stopped smoking, but it was too late. He deteriorated dramatically and died on September 1, 1981. A week later our approval to emigrate came through.

If my wedding had been a challenge for my mother, her husband's funeral was far more difficult. He was no longer there in support and now she was the centre of attention, with a large crowd of mourners including numerous ex-colleagues of my father's. Again, she survived, but survival was getting noticeably harder for her.

It was an extremely tense time for my wife and I too. I was now my mother's main means of support, but we had our hands full with three children aged under four, not to mention the prospect of emigration. My mother knew we wanted to go to Australia but we didn't talk about it. Not at such a difficult time. So English.

When our notice of approval for Australia arrived only a few days after my father had gasped his last breath, it gave us no more than one year to make the move. We decided we would stick to our plan and still go. Our career prospects were much better in Australia, our children's prospects were much better and the sunnier climate was a major attraction. But how to break this to my mother?

We didn't want to tell her until after Christmas. Her first Christmas without my father was going to be hard enough without adding the burden of our impending departure to Australia. So we told her after Christmas. It was like a second death for her. No, she wasn't interested in living in Australia. No, she would never be able to write to us.

It was the hardest decision of my life. We firmly believed that it was the best move for our family, and so it proved, but we understood how hard this would be for my mother. She had lost her husband and now her only child too. There was no easy solution.

As it turned out, she did write to us, at least once a month, and she wrote well, even though, when my father was alive, he had always been the family scribe. But she defied all attempts to coax her into moving. Those letters —I wrote almost every week — could never fully substitute for our physical presence but they did enable us to have a closer relationship in some ways than we would have done making occasional visits to Eastbourne.

We had another child soon after emigrating and all six of us travelled back to England for the first time three years after leaving

England. We spent most of that trip's six weeks with my mother, including taking her with us to the Isle of Wight for a few days, but we were now an invading army. Without my father, she was leading a solitary life, connecting with only a handful of people and having occasional visits from a childhood friend and her husband. Suddenly being in the company of us six set her nerves jangling.

There were one or two flare-ups. She didn't like her room in the house that we rented from a friend on the Isle of Wight and we weren't exactly relaxed travelling with four children under the age of seven. But we all survived. There were further regular return trips, usually me and one child. Much later there was a visit from our youngest with his wife, two children and in-laws. That was the first time my mother had seen her great-grandchildren.

When my mother fell and broke her wrist, our youngest daughter volunteered, without being asked, to spend two weeks with her looking after her and she brought back from her walks into town tales of people she'd met and to whom she'd chatted. Such social upfrontery, the sort my mother would have known in the East End, was a welcome splash of colour for her and she loved the stories our daughter told her. It inspired my mother to share stories of her own life with her granddaughter. It was a very precious two weeks.

My mother also had a special opportunity to know our second daughter who lived in London for a number of years and frequently saw her. Our other two children had less opportunity to spend time with her but, as with all four grandchildren, my mother revelled in these adult additions to her family. Best of all, for her 80th birthday, all my family gathered in Eastbourne and celebrated with a special lunch in her favourite restaurant.

A year later she had a series of falls and her GP said that it wasn't safe for her to continue living alone at home in her flat. He arranged for her to go into a nursing home, a move she had often sworn she would only ever make "over my dead body" but now she accepted that she had no option.

Our oldest daughter travelled from Perth to join her twin sister there and they comforted my mother, who had been placed in an establishment where the level of care was poor. I followed my daughter over and together we set about finding a better care home for her.

We found one and moved her. This proved to be her final "home". Our oldest daughter had to return to Australia and my wife then joined me for an extended stay. Belatedly, my mother had been diagnosed not long before with lung cancer and when told that if she wanted to see another Christmas, she would need to have her lungs drained for a second time, she declined. Assured that we would stay with her, she accepted that death was just days away. Her fear of dying alone was banished and she died two weeks before Christmas 2012.

We had been in contact with the only two surviving members of her family, her longtime hairdresser, whom she regarded as a daughter, and her only other surviving friend. But my wife and London-based daughter were the only ones who attended her funeral. Our other children watched on from Australia via the internet. It was a cold and bleak winter's day, with a leaden sky and sodden turf and a deathly wind. Not the kind of final send-off that any of us would choose.

It wasn't that my mother was unlikeable. Far from it. The trouble was she had led such a solitary life since my father's death that very few people knew her. She had faded from this world like the weather-beaten engraving on an old tombstone.

Now, on her 100th birthday, I think about the anonymity of her final years. She was a woman who had been part of a close-knit, thriving community growing up in the East End of London but she had been undone by life and became afraid of it. Now she lies unvisited in that cemetery which I will forever remember as it was on that miserable December day of her funeral. She is not only unvisited but permanently at rest in a town where she lived for more than 30 years without making a lasting mark.

But then who among us makes such a mark? When the vast majority of us die, our immediate family and friends (those who outlive us) will think of us, maybe read something about us. Our children and their families may gather at our graveside and say some prayers but when they, too, have gone and their children have gone, we will be lost in the mists of time. Those mists will never lift. There will be no one left who knew us or knew of us.

It's the fate that awaits everyone except truly famous and significant people but even most of today's superstars will eventually be forgotten.

The other day I pulled out copies of the obituaries I have written for the newspaper where I spent the final 27 years of my career. One stood out. Robyn was just 47 when she died of cancer. In the beautiful photo of her, she is smiling radiantly. She wasn't famous. She was an early childhood teacher. I quoted various relatives, colleagues and ex-students who talked about what a wonderful teacher she was, her lovely nature and dedication, and how she "made all the difference in our lives through our precious time at pre-school".

Teachers, more than most, have the ability to be a huge influence on young lives. But even they, even Robyn, will not earn a permanent place in the history books. They lived, they inspired many and were greatly loved but within 50-100 years of their death no one will speak of them or know they ever existed beyond being a name on a family tree growing on the internet.

Yes, although it's sad that our lives disappear like a footprint washed away on the beach by the tide, the beach remains — as do we. I believe it is not the end of our story when we die but to see light at the end of death's dark tunnel takes spiritual or religious conviction. I have come to believe that my mother and my father live on in the next world. Even though our "footprint" will perhaps remain for just a few years in this world before it vanishes, our souls journey on through the worlds of God taking to the next world our deeds and the essence of who we were in this life.

On this auspicious day, when I mourn the passing of the mother in whose womb I first formed, I find myself thinking as much about what our lives prepare us for in death. I think about where my mother is now and where all of us are headed. Some of the things we have done may hinder our progress along our path towards God; our good deeds will accelerate that progress. The sacrifices we made, the services we rendered others, the love we gave — these are riches that have no material dimensions and are not confined to this earthly existence. They do not die when the last of those who knew us die.

Just as a foetus grows and takes human shape in the world of the womb and then is born into the world beyond the mother's womb, similarly our death is also a birth, this time out of our physical bodies into another realm of existence. Just as a lot will depend after someone's birth on how well they fared as a baby in the womb, our whole time on Earth is a process of growth as we hopefully accumulate the qualities and virtues that will serve us well in the next world, where our souls are destined to continue our journey.

So instead of mourning the vicissitudes of this world, with its disappointments and losses, and the seeming insignificance of our existence, based on how quickly we will be forgotten after our death, perhaps we would be better served looking forward to the promise of the life after we die.

Of course, no one can prove conclusively that there is life after death. The closest you can get is to have faith in the teachings of someone whose claim to be a messenger of God is credible to you — in effect, God speaking through them. If you don't believe in

God, it is that much harder to open yourself up to accepting the possibility that scientific "proof" alone or the behaviour of followers of religion are insufficient reasons for denying the existence of that Greater Power we call God. Adding difficulty is the tendency these days for people to be fierce in defending the certainty of their views and equally fiercely attacking those of others.

I am puzzled how people can be so sure that God doesn't exist. Even the most brilliant of human minds totally fail to explain where the universe comes from and how everything fits together so methodically. Such things are beyond human comprehension and yet, despite that, many of us intuitively "know" with apparent certainty that there is no God.

My mother believed in God but was not religious. I never asked her what she thought about the possibility of life after death, one of many conversations I wish now that I had had with both my parents. There are many interesting conversations waiting for us in the next world — especially with those who swore blind that God and life after death were fantasies.

Until then, Mum, is there any chance you could drop me a hint about what it's like "up there"?

BIRTH OF A NEW ERA

I AM OFF to an ominous start. With my wife pregnant for the first time, I dutifully attend an antenatal class at our local hospital. And I almost faint. It isn't a good sign for how I'll fare with the real thing.

Fast-forward to a month before Fiona's due date. She's been in hospital for two weeks with high blood pressure. She badly wants to get out of the hospital and is going quietly crazy with nothing to do but wait for the daily blood pressure check. When the reading comes down, she can go home, which she desperately wants to do. The constant encouragement from nurses to "just relax" ensures that, if anything, her blood pressure's going up, not down.

There is some welcome distraction for her that morning when the doctor decides to send Fiona for an X-ray so he can check the position of the baby. He thinks it may be in a breach position. In those days scans weren't done automatically and this was to be the first look inside of her pregnancy.

That day I'm at work in London editing the W.H. Smith staff newspaper and I'm close to deadline. Just after lunch, my wife phones me. "Guess what," she says. I flippantly reply absolutely without the benefit of any inside information: "You're having twins."

"Yes, and they're coming now!"

Incredibly, I don't faint. Not even close to it. I am suddenly transformed into Daddy Cool. I calmly knock on my manager's door, calmly interrupt his meeting with a senior member of staff and calmly announce that I will have to go because my wife is in labour with twins. They're both more stunned than me. The shock hasn't registered with me yet.

So I head off to St Pancras and catch a train for the 20-minute journey to St Albans. My train arrives on time, which is more than can be said for the twins. They might even have arrived while I was on the train but at least the journey gives me a chance to try and get my head around this unexpected turn of events. As if I could do that in just 20 minutes. Try 20 years.

What had happened was that when Fiona's waters broke and she could feel all sorts of gymnastics going on inside her, she suggested that the doctor should look at the X-ray taken just a couple of hours earlier. "Oh, yes, that's a good idea," the doctor said.

A nurse duly went off to see the radiologist who confirmed that there wasn't just one baby in there but two. One much bigger than the other. The X-ray drew every available doctor and nurse on duty that day eager to behold this sensational news.

Back on the ward, the doctor delivered the news when he returned to Fiona's bedside and announced: "Congratulations, you're having twins!"

She was unsurprisingly even more stunned than the doctor. In a kind of haze, she asked for the phone and rang me. Then she rang her mother but got no further than "Mum, sit down, I've got some news for you. I'm having twins," and the phone went dead. Fiona thought her mother had passed out. But it was nothing worse than the line cutting out. Maybe even God was shocked at the news.

When I rang my mother, she was so thrown by the news that she put sugar instead of salt into the peas she was cooking.

Now it's almost 2.30 in the morning and after the longest evening of our lives, the first twin is about to be born. I am in the delivery room. Even though I haven't fainted and outwardly I still appear calm, inwardly I'm … let's not go there.

Gemma is the first out. She weighs just 2lb 12oz (1.3kg) and barely fills the midwife's hand. The paediatrician, arriving only minutes before the birth, whisks Gemma off to a contraption that looks like a toaster. It's going to be touch and go whether she will survive at that weight.

Five minutes later her 6lb (2.7kg) sister, Anna, somehow is born. Fiona was only 8cm dilated for Gemma's birth and for Anna that is a dangerous squeeze. In addition, she is a breach birth and gets stuck on the way out. The result is that she's not much healthier than Gemma. She's got respiratory problems, jaundice and a broken collarbone.

The survival of both of them is in the balance. We are told that the next 48 hours will be vital. But they make it.

We learnt afterwards that although they were identical twins and there was only one placenta, Gemma didn't get her fair share of sustenance in the womb and didn't develop as fully as she needed to before being born. Today a problem like that can be fixed in the early stages of pregnancy. Anna was in hospital for three weeks and Gemma for seven. Even after those seven weeks, Gemma still weighed only 5lb (2.3kg).

While it was a very rough and traumatic entry into the world for both of them and such a long separation from each other in the hospital — no way for twins to begin life — that period did give us a chance to prepare for a double homecoming. With Fiona going into hospital so early, we had not even got all that we needed for the one child that we thought we were going to have. So we had some urgent shopping to do to fully equip ourselves for two babies.

Forty-five years later, there is still a difference in size between them and although they are identical twins, it's fairly easy to tell who's who. Only once or twice have we been stumped trying to work out which one's Anna and which one's Gemma in a photograph.

Both have had quite a few health challenges, all probably related to their difficult gestations and births. Anna has suffered from breathing difficulties and panic attacks and Gemma has had arthritis from an early age.

So you'd think that, after such a traumatic experience with this first pregnancy and births, we would be sworn off having any more children. Don't you believe it. We were seized by a kind of madness because just 19 months later our third child, Natalie, was born and a further three and a half years later we had our fourth, Philip. Four in five years.

Both Natalie and Philip arrived without the same degree of drama as their big sisters. Still, neither birth was without its moments of tension. Fiona was only 8cm dilated when Natalie was born and she was told not to push while in full-on labour with Philip because the doctor was delayed getting to the hospital. As a GP, he was still finishing off his morning surgery. To add to the fun, Philip arrived with his umbilical cord wrapped around his neck and his hand on his head.

I guess life was never meant to be easy.

FLOWER POWER

WHAT'S NOT TO like about flowers? They are the essence of beauty. Extolled by painters and poets who have even been moved to venerate the humble daffodil and a simple vase of flowers. Yet I have had a troubled relationship with flowers.

On more than one occasion, my wife has accused me of never giving her any flowers. She exaggerates, of course, but her wild claim has its origins in a tactless moment of mine during the first month of our marriage. I had been on a work trip to the Denby Pottery Company and decided I would prove my undying love by buying her ... a set of Denby plates.

Ouch. That gesture did not go down well. If ever I should have chosen flowers, this was the time. The Barbra Streisand-Neil Diamond song, You Don't Bring Me Flowers, could have been written for me.

But this summer it has been another song which has come to mind when I think about my difficult relationship with flowers — Peter Paul and Mary's 1962 hit, Where Have All the Flowers Gone? Indeed, where have all the flowers in my garden gone?

A few weeks ago, before summer really fired up, they were flourishing. Flowers differed enthusiastically in kind, colour, form and shape. Not quite as dazzling as one front garden round the corner from me but, considering the minimal effort I had put into our front garden, it was impressive enough to turn heads. Even the grass was green, no mean achievement for me.

Now, the inevitable onslaught of hot weather has claimed many of the flowers. Some of those remaining are wilting, almost everything in the once-vibrant garden is struggling and only a few blooms refuse to bend. My two hanging baskets, once so proudly decorative on the verandah, are hanging their heads in shame. I guess my fingers just aren't a deep enough green.

But nothing in this world lasts forever except possibly the media's obsession with tall poppies — which they cultivate and then kill off, like the flowers in my garden. No, the truth is we all have to accept that where there is life, there is also death. So I have been thinking of the garden as a microcosm of my life and the flowers as people who have brought me happiness but are now dead, either literally or in the sense of my having lost contact with them.

When my garden started to lose its gloss, it was coming on Christmas and every year at that time I play Greg Lake's dark song, I Believe in Father Christmas. It's not exactly Jingle Bells jollity but it's my favourite Christmas song and it's almost 50 years old. Lake, who first caught my eye in 1970s supergroup Emerson, Lake & Palmer, passed away all of six years ago. One of many flowers in my life that have "gone to graveyards, everyone".

Every time I check the Guardian newspaper's obituary pages, I find another flower from my youth has died. Often they are entertainers or sportsmen. Footballer George Cohen and actress Ruth Madoc, for example — both gone just before Christmas. But their passing takes me back to the landscape I once shared with them and in which they were standout flowers.

Cohen was the right back in England's one and only World Cup-winning team of 1966. That day my parents and I hurried back from our holiday on the Isle of Wight to sit in front of our black and white TV to watch the final, the tensest two hours of my life. I can still recite the names of all 11 members of that team.

Madoc was the holiday camp announcer who greeted everyone over the public address with "Hello, campers, hi-de-hi" in the much-loved (certainly by my family) British sitcom Hi-De-Hi. That was first on TV in February 1981, just a few months after my wife, twin daughters and I had stayed for the one and only time at a holiday camp, with my parents babysitting nervously for us in the evenings. Just seven months after Hi-De-Hi made its debut, my father died. He only ever knew our first three children as babies and never got to meet our fourth.

Just two of the hundreds of flowers that once had starring roles in my summer garden.

Then there are friends who have long since passed away. Joe was my best friend at school, half English and half Chinese, and the only one with whom I ever really stayed in contact after I left in 1969. He died young of lung cancer many years ago. He was one of the first and most exotic flowers to die.

The unknown fates of others who were once important parts of my life amount to a sort of death as well. For example, Annette, my first girlfriend in 1970, or Dave, the guy who introduced me to the Bahá'í Faith in 1971. Flowers that have long since disappeared from my imagined garden.

But hold on a moment. I don't want to wallow and drown in a sea of nostalgia, dragging out long-lost girlfriends, favourite teachers, sporting heroes, flamboyant aunts and bombastic bosses. It's

OK to glance backwards but not to stare at the past to the exclusion of both the present and the future.

The garden will bloom again, new flowers will hopefully replace old ones. The question is: how beautiful will my garden — indeed humanity's garden — look this year? How hard are we all prepared to work on growing a new array of flowers? Making the garden even more beautiful than last time?

I'm aiming high and this quote from sacred writings is my inspiration: " ... *although we are of different individualities, different in ideas and of various fragrances, let us strive like flowers of the same divine garden to live together in harmony.*"

As with any garden, it will need innovation and graft. Rather than sticking with the tried and trusted, there will be greater beauty in embracing new possibilities, discovering new flowers and blending everything together in new combinations.

We can still draw on past inspirations. Old flowers can bloom again, brighter and more redolent than before. Just this month I have twice experienced this.

Listening for the first time in many years to the music of Laura Nyro, I found a depth and beauty in her work that I had never appreciated before. As well, my wife and I met up again by chance with two long-lost friends and three hours of free-flowing conversation kindled a new kind of friendship.

These are just two minor examples and there are plenty of much more significant things we can do to create a garden worthy of our most ambitious imaginations.

We just have to take time to smell the roses and maybe invest our future garden with the kind of creativity that produced Monet's water lilies or Van Gogh's irises. Only this garden will not be a celebration of just one flower, such as a host of golden daffodils, but a sensuous mixture of many.

FUNNY BUSINESS

A FUNNY THING happened to me on a sunny summer's day in the late 1990s, while on holiday visiting the Valley of the Giants at Walpole. Leaving the treetop walk, my wife and I were chatting while, at the same time, keeping the eye in the back of our heads on our four kids as they messed around in our wake. Subjects often get buried in the dark blur of everyday family life and emerge blinking into the daylight while on holiday. One such subject surfaced on that walk. We wondered how some long-lost friends of ours were doing. The conversation was along the lines of: "We haven't seen or heard from them in about 10 years … Their three kids must all be at high school now … We should try and catch up with them this year."

Moments later, as we walked along the footpath, appearing from around the corner in front of us was Keith McDonald and his family. No, not my hologram but Perth's "other" Keith McDonald. The one we had just been talking about. And with him were his wife, Judi, and their children.

Freaky or what? But our friendship with these other McDonalds is full of freakishness.

The friendship started in 1985. I was doing some freelance writing for a local music magazine and in those prehistoric, pre-online banking days the editor paid me by sending a cheque in the post.

Only on this occasion he sent it to the wrong address — to the well-known local musician and star of the kids' TV show Fat Cat, Keith McDonald. Judi, who's a woman with a clear sense of right and wrong, knew that it wasn't meant for her husband, even though they could easily have claimed it as their own. She tracked me down to hand the cheque over to its rightful owner.

She rang me at the newspaper where I worked and we agreed it would be nice for our two families to meet up rather than just put the cheque in the post. So one Sunday, at Fremantle Esplanade, the four Big Macs and six Little Macs met for the first time. Yes, it was only six Little Macs — two of theirs and four of ours — because Judi was pregnant at the time with her third child.

While the kids all played happily in the park, we adults shared stories about our lives and that's when we discovered some very freaky coincidences. These went way beyond the fact that both our surnames were spelled the right way (big "M", no "a", small "c", capital "D"). Keith's dad was Frank. So was mine. Keith's birthday was December 27. Mine was December 26, although I was born a year earlier than him. And Judi told us that their unborn child was going to be a boy, their only son, and they had chosen the name, Philip, for him. Our son, also our only son, is, you guessed, Philip.

But Keith and I agreed that in one important way we had nothing in common. He couldn't write and I couldn't sing.

We did, however, combine our different skills on three occasions. First, I wrote an article in 1999 for The West Australian Magazine about us. It told of the freaky coincidences and then went on to talk at greater length about Keith's life after Fat Cat.

He was still playing pub gigs but he had also developed a musical education program which he was taking to schools around the

State. For the article, I went to see him in action at Padbury Primary School. And guess where you will find that school: Macdonald Avenue. Only it misspelled the name of the avenue (M-a-c, small "d", o-n-a-l-d).

The second and third times we joined forces were when my two youngest children got married. I wrote the words and Keith wrote the tunes for songs about both couples. The first of these in 2004, The Ballad of Philip and Naomi, told a freaky true story of its own.

Philip met his future wife after flying with his sister, Natalie to London. On the plane Natalie got talking — boy, can she talk, I don't know where she gets it from — to the elderly gentleman, Nick, sitting next to her. When she finally fell asleep, Philip got a chance to have a conversation of his own with Nick.

It turned out that Nick was quite nervous about finding his way through Heathrow on his own, so my two kids offered to accompany him to public transport (what well-brought-up children they are!).

They exchanged contact details with Nick and a few weeks later, when he returned to Perth, he got in touch with Philip, saying that he had a lovely great niece and he encouraged Philip to go on a blind date with her.

Philip, then 19, had never had a girlfriend and he nearly lost this one before even meeting her because he turned up at The Dome in Fremantle on his motorbike. That put Nick's great-niece right off. But they survived that first big setback and two years later Naomi and Philip were married with "Uncle Nick" the guest of honour and Keith performing our song about their romance.

We catch up with Keith and Judi two or three times a year and often enjoy Judi's gourmet cooking, which makes us nervous to invite them over to our place for lunch because no gourmet cooks live here.

Judi was also in a book club which I co-founded and ran for more than 10 years. Ever the blunt Yorkshire woman, she once gave her thumbs-down verdict on a book entitled Veronica Decides to Die by saying it should have been called Veronica Deserves to Die.

I've had only one other so-called "funny" experience. That was in the early 1970s when I knew of the Bahá'í Faith but had not yet become a Bahá'í. I travelled on my own to Edinburgh one summer for the Edinburgh Fringe Festival, where I discovered that the Fringe newspaper wanted people to review shows. I volunteered and was sent to a daytime performance of a musical.

It featured a cast of maybe 20 or 30 but there were only three of us in the audience ... and the other two left at halftime.

Anyway, I digress. The point of this tale is that when I got on the train to travel back to London, I walked almost the length of the 12 carriages looking for a vacant window seat before finally finding one.

I sat down and started reading a Bahá'í book, which I had taken with me. An hour or so later, as we neared Newcastle Upon Tyne, the elderly woman opposite me inquired what I was reading. I held it up to show her and she nodded knowingly.

This American woman, Sybil, had been a Bahá'í longer than I had been alive. She was almost certainly the only Bahá'í on a train with maybe 400 or 500 passengers and I had chosen to sit opposite her. She, too, was taken aback because she had reserved a seat but for some unknown reason cancelled it and ended up choosing to sit where I found her.

A couple of years later, when I married — by which time, with some help from Sybil, I was a Bahá'í — she flew from Illinois to London for the wedding. She died a few months later.

By the way, to this day, I still get asked occasionally if I am the Keith McDonald who used to appear on TV with Fat Cat or, on meeting someone for the first time, I introduce myself as "not the guy who used to do Fat Cat". And musician Keith often used to get asked if he was now writing for the local paper, something misguidedly thought of as more respectable than singing for a living.

I MUST GO DOWN TO THE SEA AGAIN

I AM AT South Beach. It's summer and the sun has been up for an hour. There are a group of Italian nonnas, a fossicker is standing in the water with a metal detector and assorted elderly gents in budgie smugglers are striding purposely along the water's edge talking their way from one end of the beach to the other.

The beach bends gently in a 300m arc. Sand dunes sit uneasily on the back of the beach's 30-metre strip of fine white sand. Stone groynes stand guard at both ends of the arc, jutting a short distance into the sea. The sea itself stretches languidly out to meet the clear blue sky. There's barely a ripple on the surface. The sun, half an hour after rising, has broken over the city behind the beach to pour its light onto the sea. A lone plane crawls like an insect across the sky.

I wade into the water and rub shoulders (and arms and legs and chest) with what feels like every stinger in the Indian Ocean. Stingers are one of the many hazards when wandering into their marine domain. Thankfully, I have never seen any sharks here but I have often seen crabs among the rocks at the groynes and, worse, one underneath me as I arrive invitingly overhead like an UberEats delivery. There was also the time I came face-to-face with a seal and departed the water doing a passable impression of Usain Bolt. This day, however, the stingers can't intimidate me. I treat every brushing encounter with them as nothing worse than a nip. It even adds to my sense of exhilaration. Not only have I heroically got myself out of bed early and flung myself even more heroically into the sea, but I am also heroically taking everything the stingers can throw at me, without flinching.

Thirty minutes later, I head back to my towel on the beach, car keys still safely secured under the towel, and dry off. As I do so, I watch a woman at the water's edge, arms outstretched high above her head thanking her creator for this place. Not today, but quite often, there will be someone sitting cross-legged on the beach meditating. Despite the glorious ocean, the conditions are not ideal for prayer and meditation because the smell of the beach café frying bacon in a sea of boiling fat drifts through the air, but the sun is pouring down and spiritual pores, including mine, are definitely open.

After departing the changing rooms (if you can call a building with no roof and an open shower a room), I grab my prayer book from the car and, armed with a bottle of water, head for a grassed area far from the madding crowd and smell of bacon. There I sit on a limestone wall looking out to sea and pray.

At work later that day, I have 10 times more energy and vitality than I did the day before when I didn't make it to the beach first thing. The pure physical act of swimming has invigorated me. Not that I am any kind of Ian Thorpe. I've never had swimming lessons and I am a late convert to swimming in the ocean. I always stick close to the shore, away from the sharks, only to beach myself occasionally as I struggle to move with dignity through six-inch-deep water. But it doesn't matter how fast you swim or how good you are. Just being in the water and swimming, in itself, is invigorating.

Nevertheless, even I struggle to recognise myself doing this early morning routine of getting up at 6 o'clock, going down to the beach, swimming and then sitting around afterwards saying prayers. My younger self would never have considered doing anything like this.

I first started my ocean swims when I was in my 50s and just a year or two later I particularly remember arriving at the beach one specific summer morning. It was January 2005 and the Boxing Day tsunami a few weeks earlier was on my mind. I got to thinking about how, hovering on another of this ocean's shorelines that Boxing Day morning, I could have been swept to my death by a tsunami of such power it demolished everything in its path for maybe 15km and claimed at least 225,000 lives. But here I was on a benign shore.

Like others drawn to the meeting of sea and shore at dawn, I dropped my things on the sand and just stood and gazed. The sea has that effect on people and Bahá'u'lláh's words about the ocean came to mind:

O wayfarer in the path of God! Take thou thy portion of the ocean of His grace and deprive not thyself of the things that lie hidden in its depths ...

I stared out to sea in a kind of trance. It was just the intoxication of the sea. There was some mysterious force drawing me to this dawning place of natural wonder. Although, on the surface, nothing seemed to be happening, I knew that even this small portion of the mighty ocean, framed in the view from this beach, supported countless numbers of sea dwellers which invisibly went about their journeys. I didn't need to see them to prove that they were there. The next day they might well have moved on elsewhere and a new cast of anonymous, invisible creatures would be entertaining themselves.

I considered, too, how the water now lapping at my feet could travel great distances on the currents in just a single day so who could know where it was yesterday or when the tsunami had hit? How little we know. Although every morning the ocean was there, it wasn't the same water or the same marine inhabitants. It never stopped moving, changing and evolving. The same, yet totally different.

I imbibed its mysteries; imagined myself plunging beneath the surface to find what lay hid in its depths. Plunging into those words of Baha'u'lláh's, I assured myself how, through grace, I lived and continued to marvel at the serenity of the ocean, while, through that same grace, thousands of others had died in this same ocean as a result of the tsunami and obtained a serenity beyond human comprehension in the next world. Beyond the deepest depths of any ocean.

Who could know why some lived and some died? No one could answer this but, standing at the edge of the sea with an ocean of awe flooding into my chest, this scene was enough of an answer for me, even though it told me only that there was a far greater power at play than anything I could muster. A power that was capable of both beauty and horror.

I had too many earthly commitments to dally long at the beach, so experience of the ocean was limited accordingly that day. But, feeling a rush of wonderment at the breathtaking serenity of the ocean and all that lay hid within it — so different from the day of the tsunami — I peeled off my shirt, kicked off my shoes and plunged into the water. Absolution. Cleansing. Purification. Holy water, untainted by the demands of the day to come.

Returning to that quote, it continues:

... Be thou of them that have partaken of its treasures. A dewdrop out of this ocean would, if shed upon all that are in the heavens and on the earth, suffice to enrich them with the bounty of God, the Almighty, the All-Knowing, the All-Wise.

ABOUT THE AUTHOR

Keith McDonald was a print journalist for 44 years. He started as a cadet on The Croydon Advertiser, his local paper, in South London, England and ended with 27 years as a reporter, feature writer, section editor, columnist and sub-editor with The West Australian, a daily newspaper. As a volunteer, he has also edited three national Bahá'í publications. He has been married for 49 years and has four children and eight grandchildren. He has been a Bahá'í for 50 years.

ACKNOWLEDGEMENTS

My grateful thanks to:

Fiona, Anna, Emily, Lisa, Michael, Laksar, Janet and Coral for being brave enough to give me honest feedback.

Elaine, Rachman and their Storycatcher writing group for inspiring me to keep going.

My family for constantly telling me that I'm a good writer.

Stephen for making this book look good.

Lidia for fixing my mistakes.